Bonneville
Blue

Bonneville Blue

JOAN CHASE

Farrar Straus Giroux

New York

Copyright © 1991 by Joan Chase
All rights reserved
Printed in the United States of America
Designed by Victoria Wong
First edition, 1991

Library of Congress Cataloging-in-Publication Data
Chase, Joan.
Bonneville blue / Joan Chase. — 1st ed.
p.   cm.
I. Title.
PS3553.H3346B6   1991
813'.54—dc20   90-28551   CIP

I am grateful to The Guggenheim Foundation for its support and I want to thank David Huddle, Alan Broughton, John Engels, Mary Jane Dickerson, Margaret Edwards, and Bernice Rabe for invaluable encouragement and assistance. As always, thanks to Ellen, Jonathan, Hayden, and Alec.

To Kaye and Larry

Contents

Bonneville Blue

IRENE WHACKED the bejesus out of the sofa cushions, snatched her sun hat, and in shorts and sling backs sailed out the door for the Heart Fund. Her own daddy had died of a heart attack, but still, when the woman asked her to canvass, a flat refusal was on the tip of her tongue—until the draft evader across the way straggled out to his car and she reconsidered. Somebody around here could march for something worthwhile that didn't involve burning a draft card or the American flag. She'd come to regret the impulse, though, the little cardboard box, decorated with a lopsided heart, sitting on top of the refrigerator for two weeks nagging at her. Today she was determined to get the job under way. She'd do half the units in the court and be back before Freddy came to. Every day he fought his nap like a hanging and then on the other side could scarcely be raised to life. He was a trying and ornery child, but Irene wouldn't have wished his home life on a heathen. No wonder he was prone to nosebleeds, picking everything in sight, and his fingernails bitten to the quick. Any bit of decent upbringing she would give him was all to the good, whether he had the sense to appreciate it or not.

The September heat, rising off the asphalt parking lot in the center of the courtyard, pretty much empty of cars this time of day, urged her to bid a hasty fond farewell to the Bonneville parked—lucky for her—right at her doorstep. Get cracking to the far end of the street, where she would begin her begging, the little red ticker pulsing between her thumb and forefinger. The woman had claimed modern medicine was closing the gap, wouldn't be no time at all till folks' hearts lasted a lifetime. She'd said to Irene, like a diviner, didn't she want to help save her husband, men in their prime the first to go? If Irene could help Big Jim, she figured any amount of marching and self-abasement would be worth the effort. Even knocking on strangers' doors, something she couldn't remember doing in her whole life. Except one time when she had a flat, and that was down home, where folks were sociable once you got past the dogs. All she had to do was get started and plow on to the finish, and considering the houses she intended to skip right past, for any number of reasons, there'd be nothing to it. Like Big Jim said, she knew how to make the fur fly.

Mercifully, there was no answer at the unit closest to the main road—check that one off. Her own heart had kicked up so violently, her raps on the metal screen door came back at her like an echo. She pinched herself and muttered, "Settle down, girl," forced a brief laugh, and moved on along the row, passing up a house in between where she'd seen the draft evader visit. Sissy lived next door, and of course she was home, plunked in front of the television. Irene scratched on the window screen and Sissy's head spun around, her eyes no bigger or any different in color from the enormous freckles that plastered her face. Looking to Irene like a peacock, its tail with a million eyes.

Sissy, yawning and stretching, beckoned her inside, reaching over to turn down the fan. When she saw the little box Irene carried, she gave her the eyebrow, eyes spinning. "I never figured y'all for no do-gooder."

"I do good at some things." Irene shook her hips and Skinny-Minny shimmied back.

"Set down while I find you something. I bet this all goes straight to the government."

Irene felt herself redden as if somehow she was to blame. "I don't have nothing to give nobody yet. The woman couldn't get her regular gal, so I said I'd help her out."

Sissy scraped change from the bottom of her pocketbook while Irene looked off, examining the overflowing laundry basket waiting by the door. Sissy didn't have a machine of her own, using the laundromat at night when her husband came home with the car. If he came home. The winter before, he'd admitted having an affair, no surprise to Irene. At the annual New Year's party you always knew when it was midnight, Harry's tongue in your mouth.

"That'll do." Irene held out the box. Sissy was too generous for her own good. "Just give 'em enough to keep 'em quiet."

Sissy dropped in some coins. "I always thought that was the way to go. Drop in your tracks and count yourself lucky." She shook the box, handing it back to Irene. "Don't say I never give you nothing."

Irene shrugged. That kind of joking was part of taking their money, she figured—as though she might embezzle the Heart Fund. She grinned at Sissy, inviting her to come visit, heading back into the heat. Irene recalled that when her own washer went on the blink, Sissy took her clothes out to save Irene the bother, and then Irene couldn't get her to take a cent. Instead of counting up what Sissy put in the box, Irene wrote out a dollar on the receipt and left it on the table. "Tax deductible." She winked at Sissy. If it didn't amount to that much, Irene would make up the difference herself.

Trailing in and out of the walks and doorways, Irene realized for the first time exactly how orderly the plan was, measured turns leading to every entrance, two steps up, the yard plots cut out like postage stamps. Sometime in the past the government had designed the model community—some do-gooder's notion gone to the dogs, the buildings run down, most of the neighbors hardly speaking. Although the walls were thin enough. Every morning when you went into your medicine cabinet, you could have whispered, "Howdy-do."

She was bound to avoid the next house and went stiffly past in the heeled sandals to minimize their clicking. Anna lived there with her ragamuffin boy and that poor excuse for a husband. He worked steady, something to do with the colored, but Irene wouldn't have asked them for the world's last dime. Anna was out-and-out crazy, and he put up with her, wearing a shit-eating grin, like she was his little joke on the rest of them. Irene already knew more than was decent, and none of it funny, because Anna made regular treks to her end of the courtyard to visit Jessie, Irene's next-door neighbor. Traipsing all that way, as if she wouldn't rest until every last one of them got a glimpse of the devastation to come.

Right then, in her glimpse, the Bonneville shimmered powdery-blue in the sun, far off in front of her own home, and gave her strength. In that setting, it stuck out like an orchid pinned on a pauper. Even the few neat and painted houses in any row only showed the rest as more neglected. Above them, the siren at the corner municipal building aimed like a gigantic ear trumpet for a God who was hard of hearing.

The icy touch on her arm startled Irene, and with Anna so close beside her, the box in her hand began to quiver as though a live heart was trapped inside. Anna held out coins, her open pocketbook clutched at her bosom. Irene let her take the box. She didn't care if that was the last she saw of it, her eyes fixed on Anna's feet, awash in the tied shoes of a large man, hobo-style. When Anna gave back the box, Irene, in her rush to be gone, forgot about the receipt altogether, flustered to hear Anna's thank-you. She wasn't doing anything special, asking folks for their hard-earned money, fouling up the receipts. Anna could save her thanks for the cootie-catcher.

The shoes reminded her, got her all confused. When Irene was at her own house and Anna passed by, no matter how peculiar she looked or acted, Irene could have said "Boo!" But alone in unknown territory, she wasn't herself at all. The old colored woman had worn shoes like that when Irene, a girl of fifteen, met her by the flour mill in a part of town where she'd never been. Irene gave her the money and she counted it out before she took Irene to the doctor, who was white enough, like she'd been told, and he'd done what was needed and ended the trouble. Though the fear had lasted over twenty years and could follow her two hundred miles distant and into the middle of a day.

Anna still gaping after her, Irene fought down running off and walked on to the first house on the next row. There a woman she'd never seen before invited her to come inside and sit down, thanking her openly for being charitable. She gave Irene two dollars like it was her pleasure to do so. Irene had to ask her how to spell out Klinkenburg for the receipt and the woman had laughed that nobody could spell that name, or believe it either, a good-natured pretty woman with sheer white dimity at her windows. Maybe they'd meet again and get acquainted, Irene was thinking, until the woman said it was lucky she was at home. Generally she was at work. A lot of the houses were empty during the day, one after another of the women taking jobs, children pawned off on the few who stayed behind to keep a real home going. When she left, Mrs. Klinkenburg said she hoped to see Irene again, but Irene wouldn't hold her breath. She remembered from school how chummy some girls could be one day, cut you dead the next.

Anna had vanished by then, and Irene tried two more houses where no one answered before she decided to call it quits and head for home. The box in her hand was light as a feather, but the whole project weighed on her, as if she was down at the yard with Big Jim hauling cement. If she didn't get out again to finish up the court, she'd just fill out some receipts, make up names, put in the money herself. Or she could say she'd been sick and hand in what she had. Already she'd have to calculate what Anna gave and make out some kind of receipt. That kind of fiddling and worry was exactly why Irene didn't believe in soliciting. Next thing, you were the one with heart failure, while the folks at the Fund tolled the bell one more time.

There was the Bonneville, safe and sound. She reached out to touch it, feeling relieved. It seemed cozy as a pet, although it was about a city block long. Sometimes in the evenings, she and Big Jim sat out in the car, the dark-blue leather seats deeper than anything they had in the house, the smell brand-new because Big Jim never lit up a cigarette or allowed even a cup of coffee inside. With the radio going and the air conditioning, everything handy, it could have been a room at a resort. No wonder Big Jim thought of calling it "My Blue Heaven," and made her sing a line though she couldn't carry a tune in a bucket. Only the Saturday before, they'd sat there when they drove in from the races. Big Jim had started in tickling her in the ribs, making his love sound that was like an engine starting up, and she'd joined in with her muffler hum. It seemed they hadn't fooled around like that for a long time, like two kids, and about the time he put his hand under her jersey, she'd had to get a move on. Nothing would stop him once he got going, and he'd be lowering his head to take in the rest of her, what did he care about a street lamp. And she'd had to wrestle and tickle him back to disentangle herself, though he didn't follow her until he'd lapped the chamois one last time over the finish of the car, preserving the Saturday wash and shine.

Irene wasn't a bit different about the house, spick-and-span, her man off to work in a clean, ironed outfit, packing a lunch fit to feed a horse, enough to share all round. About once a week, everybody on his noon shift was pestering for some of her 7-Up Cake. Big Jim could go off with a free heart, knowing she would look after things. Only that morning, over his eggs and bacon he'd looked up from the paper and said, "Irene Lee, there's some crayon on them whitewalls." Right after his buddy picked him up, she scrubbed the tires with Lestoil and a stiff brush. She had her suspicions about who to blame but she'd have to catch him first or he'd only lie.

Speaking of the devil, it was time to wake up the brat. It wasn't just the tires; Freddy was kind of a full-time brat— nothing he could help. There was no example in the home, his mother slaving all day for K mart, supporting the family, including an able-bodied man who knew when he had a deal and hadn't even bothered to marry her. He was mostly in bed when he wasn't in the slammer for beating somebody up. He ought to be doing time for the way he treated Freddy. Irene could jolly up most any ol' boy, but she didn't bother with Leroy. You could figure he was in a vile humor simply because he hadn't died in the night.

Going through the dining end of her living room, Irene delivered a brisk tattoo to the wash basket, ironing sprinkled and rolled tight, neat as sausages. Mrs. Whalen, who had nothing better to do, would be after her because it hadn't been done the day before she'd left it. Some folks thought all Irene lived for was to stand over an ironing board. Besides, she was particular. Not one piece went out of the house without every seam laid flat, as if it were steamrolled—there ought to be a prize.

She'd been thinking the room felt hot, in spite of the fan, before she heard the scuffling on the front gravel and whirled about to see the door left ajar, and beyond, the draft evader slinking out of his yard. She crept over to peer out, wondering what he'd look like without his beard, probably a chin like a golf ball. A man that tall and skinny put her in mind of an African she'd seen on the television, somebody who was starving to death. He might as well be black, butting in, all the time making folks feel sorry.

Ever since the draft evader had moved into the court, a four-square arrangement of four-unit wooden row houses, Irene had felt uneasy about what belonged to her, particularly the Bonneville. Not that a coward who wouldn't land a blow for his country was any particular threat to anything, but he was bound to be envious and out of sorts. You had to wonder why he and his pals never said anything above a whisper, mumbling and snickering. Cheap housing attracted all kinds. There must have been four people going to college and some beyond college, right in those sixteen houses, the state university a stone's throw down the highway. In her own front yard, Irene couldn't carry on a simple conversation without thinking somebody might correct her English, as likely as not the swami across the way hanging out his turbans, college kids in every direction avoiding work and war.

When one young gal knocked on the door and tried to give her a pamphlet and some song and dance, Irene had interrupted, never dreaming she'd soon be going out with the Heart Fund. "I don't have time for that stuff, honey. I've got too much work to do." She said it in a loud voice too, like she wasn't a bit ashamed, and the haughty little thing had blushed before she went on. Imagine, wearing her feelings on her sleeve. Irene wanted to call after, "I don't bite." She looked out over the neighborhood, length after length of metal fencing separating this from that, glittering to the horizon. Sometimes Irene thought they might as well be locked in together there on Division Hill.

The draft evader had slipped back to his yard and was talking over the fence to the college-graduate divorcée. All that education gone for a fare-thee-well; she was one of the few women in the court who stayed at home and that was with only one little child to watch. Her ex must have been paying a pretty penny.

And for what?—couldn't be much in bed, thin like that and white as arsenic, wearing a long gingham skirt in the heat of day like she was about to milk a cow. Irene would pass her by for the Heart Fund—they had nothing in common. Maybe she would just tell the woman she didn't have time, mail the money anonymously. Or spend it on something extra for Freddy, a charity case at home. This time, going toward the stairs, she gave the ironing a swift kick, feeling every one of the half dozen little burns she regularly gave herself in her hurry, each one a blight on the fairness of her hands and arms.

Big as Freddy was, she had to deliver him bodily to the front stoop. There she propped him, yawning and peaked, like something artificial. Part of the afternoon he'd hardly stir, trying to wake up, which didn't mean there wasn't plenty of mischief in him. Since the tires were marked on, she'd have to keep him in sight, sit on him all the harder. Unless she gave up and let him wander, seeing who else he could bother. There was no way one person could make up for everything he was lacking. He hunched over the coloring book she'd picked up at the five-and-dime, no more spark to him than the Simple Simon meeting the pieman gaping back at him from the page. Though if she turned her back he'd have the papers peeled off the crayons, or dig a hole in the book, coloring his way to China. When he started biting his nails, she slapped his fingers and gave him a piece of candy. Doreen, his mother, would have given him the pacifier when he wiggled around like that, a criminal act in Irene's estimation. The child would never grow up. It was bad enough Doreen wouldn't put him in the private kindergarten, saving money on Irene. Well, she didn't mind the job that much, and sometimes she went over the alphabet with Freddy and they practiced counting. Probably his baby talk was a put-on for attention. He was definitely all right upstairs, counting on his own to a hundred. If she had time to listen, he could make a thousand.

Naptime was over all around the neighborhood, cries and giggles breaking the quiet from behind shaded windows, sounding over the hum of fans. Irene and Freddy sat unwinking like two padded figures. Then five houses down, a metal door clanged shut behind a plump blond baby who wobbled onto the stoop, his sopped diaper dragging bottom, his rosy mouth plugged with a pacifier he alternated with a nursing bottle of pale-pink fluid. "Hey there, Danny-boy," Irene burbled a smothery greeting. "Ooo got somphin good for Irene Lee?" The little mess! She loved babies, the whole kit and caboodle, although like kittens they grew into something else. Except her own two, of course, who were still her babies, although they were away from home so much now she could get herself into a dither. The week before, she'd cooked a pail of applesauce and another time forgot to cook at all. Freddy, green with envy over baby Danny, was rubbing his nose with a fist. She gave him a poisonous frown— he'd get more than he bargained for if he got blood on his clothes and she had to do a wash before he went home.

The banging door acted as a signal and the parking lot sprang to life with the afternoon crowd, newly invigorated from sleep or home from school. Irene settled against the siding of her house. She might sprawl or tease, this one or that, but she wouldn't miss a trick. Mr. Freddy would soon discover that, if he tried any monkeyshines. When she went in for a popsicle of frozen Kool-Aid, she brought a bib to tie around his neck. A few simple precautions and you didn't have to be forever fussing at a child. She brushed her hand over his head, ending with a love-pinch to his cheeks when he remembered his manners and said, "T'anks, I'ene Lee," his gaze blank on the purple ice.

Irene nodded across the courtyard to old Mrs. Wink, her ally in the thankless task of watching other women's children while they tripped off in high heels and hairdos, acting as if they could leave their worries behind. An elderly woman with arthritis, she was as grim and wary as one might suppose, eating off the government on pennies a day. Thank heaven, with Big Jim's benefits, Irene could retire before she soured on life. Still, she felt for the old soul and tried to be neighborly.

"Where's Jeanie today?" she called. That little Sadie, four years old, regularly showed the boys London and France while the old woman droned before the television. When Mrs. Wink had an attack of gout and Irene did the watching, there were no shenanigans.

The woman's face festered in antagonism. "She wants me to keep her in the bed till five." The "she" referred to the mother, who had severely scolded Mrs. Wink when she'd locked Jeanie in a closet after she wet her pants. "Don't know's how I'm s'posed to do it, a child active as that. So's they can leave her to run and lark all night. But I'm nobody to know. Only four of my own." Irene made a clucking noise. The mother should have known better. Why else spend all that time in school? Though music school was hardly the school of life. Whenever Irene heard her trudging up the keyboard, she wanted to ask her why that folderol mattered more than her own child.

"Set right here," Irene warned Freddy, pocketing the crayons and leaving him a heap of butterscotch candies instead. "I'm going over to visit Jessie." The heat was getting to her and she needed a pep-me-up: a dose of Spanish coffee. Black as sin and served in a thimble, it was guaranteed to see you through the dinner hour and into next week. Something Jessie's mother-in-law had taught her to make, the only useful thing Jessie had gotten out of her marriage, as far as Irene could tell. They shared a wall and visited besides, so Irene thought she was in a position to know. She cut Jessie a slice of Danish, contenting herself with a taste, thinking her shorts felt a good deal tighter than they had on the Fourth of July. There might be too much of a good thing, even for Big Jim, who had never complained about a handful. He always said when he saw her coming, first thing he thought of was torpedoes, and second, he hoped for a direct hit.

In Jessie's living room, Irene sat at the dinette in the eating end of the room, which was exactly like hers on the other side of the wall, Jessie's table a duplicate too, the marbleized Formica silvered instead of gilt. Another donation from the mother-in-law, who was responsible for most of the food on the table too.

Jessie, creamy-skinned and chestnut-haired, with the smile from her days as a teenage beauty queen lingering still, had captured her Spanish husband's undying love. So he said—though it seemed to have come unattached to anything else. Irene thought more than once she'd caught his eye behind the dark glasses he wore, and the times she saw him in a T-shirt, the butterfly tattoo on his bicep seemed aflutter. All well and good, but it was Jessie who had the four little boys, born within five years, three in one tiny bedroom, the baby in with her. And when the Spaniard was hungry, it was "Jump!"—a T-bone at midnight. He ate, slept, and dressed, whoo-ee did he dress! Got a trim from Jessie, who'd been doing all right when he met her, working in a salon. Then off to the waiting world. Scatter change on the table—"And don't ask me no questions, babee!"

After Jessie got done telling Irene the latest in the marriage department, she started in talking about Anna's visits—loony-tunes from down the way in her size twelves. That struck Irene with a forceful recollection of the Heart Fund. She'd meant to bring it along and hit on Jessie. A fine thing. The rate Irene was going, she'd be lucky to have a friend left in the world.

"That pitiful child." Jessie was moaning about Anna's boy. "Yesterday she was raving about how somebody was after him and she had to hide him. Then today she asks me, 'Did you ever hate your own child?' He's setting on the floor. I give him a cracker and sent him out. I reckon I've hated mine a time or two, but they don't have to hear about it. Now she's sure he's going to be drafted, and Willy's not seven years old. I don't know what to say."

Irene had plenty she could think of to say, but at the mention of the draft she felt nervous and stood up to go. She and Jessie didn't always see eye to eye, and Irene didn't have to sit still and listen to a lot of borrowed opinions: as though a simple, homey person could have the slightest notion of what went on in the minds of Commies and generals.

"Nobody takes to a war," she interrupted Jessie, who was already repeating something the draft evader had told her, something about his name going on the most-wanted list. Wishful thinking, no doubt. "But nobody's going to stop them neither, because they're natural. Natural as what-you-say—hanky-panky." She rolled her baby blues, set to leave, just as Jessie stood up, fastening her hand on Irene's arm, while together they watched Anna open the screen door. This time she'd added a paisley headscarf, as though it went with the shoes.

"They've come," Anna whispered. "I have to hide him."

"What!" Jessie lowered her voice as Anna grabbed her arm, adding softly, "Why don't you set down a minute." She laid her other hand on top of Anna's.

Irene broke the little ring-around-the-rosy circle before Anna could latch on to her, folding her arms to herself and staring at the floor. She was determined to ignore the lipstick which had run onto Anna's teeth in an orange slick, ignore Anna staring up at her. Irene was a head taller than most women and large-boned, although at that moment she felt herself dwindling to a pennyweight.

"He's a freedom fighter." Anna nodded, finding Irene's eyes. "*You* know." Now that was reaching. One trip with the Heart Fund—she had you marching, sitting in with the niggers. Wishing you had a gun. Irene didn't know exactly why, maybe she was losing her marbles too, but deliberately and elaborately, she winked.

At that Anna gasped and threw up her hands to cover her mouth, hurrying out the door. Watching her flee along the walk, bent and shaking, Irene could see Anna was laughing her head off. A moron's excitement, she reminded herself, aware that her own blush flew on her face like a flag while she and Jessie watched out the window, shaking their heads.

"The poor child." Jessie fretted about the boy Willy, wondering if Anna was upset partly because of her mother's recent death. "Well, there's upset and there's *upset*," Irene muttered, then stopped herself. But it wasn't natural, such different types of people living cheek by jowl, knowing each other's business. You could almost forget who you were supposed to be.

Jessie came to, hearing a child screeching in the yard, and she jumped for the kitchen, seizing a spatula and roaring out the door. "I've had the last bit of your nastiness," she yelled, streaming to the battlefront. Irene had to hand it to Jessie, being both mother and father. Although sometimes she thought Jessie had the patience to hang herself, still the polite good girl—who'd gone to the nuns for her schooling and, except for the Spaniard, lived like a priest at confession—listening to more sorry tales, the goings-on of adulterers and divorcées. College graduates bent on saving the world. Sometimes Irene felt a yearning to talk to Jessie herself, although she didn't know what she'd say. And besides, Jessie had troubles of her own. She nodded her head in approval when that great big baby of Jessie's, six years old, began to stamp and holler, the rest of him dark as his head. More insult than injury, if she knew Jessie.

If she was given a free hand in Vietnam, Irene thought, she could settle the whole affair in about five minutes. A divided country wasn't much different from a quarrelsome family, required the same no-nonsense handling. She'd had more than her share of strappings growing up, until the day she ran off to marry Big Jim. It was her mamma who applied the switch, and Irene bore it for the sake of her daddy, who never laid a hand on her. Even when her mamma demanded that he whip her and unspoil her, since he was the one who had done it, he took Irene away from the house until the storm blew over, sometimes treated her to a sundae in town. After he was gone, Irene walked. Hadn't gone back since.

On the way out, Irene passed Jessie on the porch, her wide-eyed baby riding her hip. "Where in tarnation did that brat get to?" Irene winked, surveying the area for Freddy. Really, she wasn't all that concerned, and she sat down on the stoop. Maybe she'd let him carry the Heart Fund, if he was so wild to be out and about.

It wasn't long before she spied him, his narrow, butched head stuck up amid the congregation of kids on tricycles, plastic airplanes, Caterpillars, and hobby horses which had drawn into a wagon train at the curb in front of Anna's. That one would always draw a crowd—out there with bingo cards and board games. A freak show herself. Sometimes Freddy came home with candy bars or money she'd handed out—until Irene read him the riot act. Anna and the seven-year-old freedom fighter were in plain sight, playing hosts, when there ought to have been a sign in the yard, QUARANTINE.

Freddy sat on a trike, its pedals unconnected to anything, legs wheeling like mad, getting nowhere—preview of the life to come. Irene didn't feel up to going after him. He could just stay put until Doreen came in from work. Then Irene wouldn't have to face him until Monday morning, the weekend to rest up. She went inside, the slant of the sun on her back like the set of an ax. Her daddy at evening led the cow into the shed for milking. Afterward there was always cream for her in the cracked mug left on the window ledge. Her beauty medicine, her daddy called it, something to keep her fat and sassy.

On Saturday morning, while they washed the car, Irene asked Big Jim, "If you was to have all the money in the world, what would you do?" He didn't cease moving the rag over the car or change his expression, accustomed to Irene's notions, the old what-if's. His handsome face was heavier about the jaw than when he was younger, although she found his manliness touched her more deeply. When sometimes on a dark highway he pushed the car over a hundred, for no reason, nobody else in sight, the two of them feeling the air and the perfect level, Irene thought that if suddenly a brick wall loomed straight ahead, she would not have blinked, taking the eternal as if it was meant to be. "You ever think of Jim-bo," she went on, after a breath, "maybe going over to the teachers' college?" Where she stood beside Big Jim, in the reflection of the car door, her stomach was set like a divan where he could rest his head. She moved off, before he'd see it. It was a relief that the willow behind him showed up just as squat.

He kept on kneeling and circled the rag. "Can't say's I have." There was finality in it and she had no idea where to go from there, not exactly certain what she meant. Jim-bo might do all right as a teacher, sure enough. He had a nice way with kids. Could be a principal one day—Big Jim's son. This time in the car door, when Big Jim stood up, they looked like a set of half-wit twins taking a bubble bath. Generally, Irene would have swung her hip, but he didn't look friendly, as if maybe he was confused. He moved on to the back of the car with the bucket and then his face sort of exploded, the rag slammed at the dirt. Irene flew to him and read GAS HOG, which was printed in large letters across the dust covering the Bonneville's sleek blue rear.

Big Jim glared at Irene. "It's getting so a man can't go off and leave with a free heart. If you're too busy setting on your fat behind to take care of things, I'll take this here car along with me."

Irene couldn't open her mouth. About as long a threat as she'd ever heard from Big Jim, the whole of it at her expense. Her first thought had been Freddy, but he barely wrote his name. Big Jim couldn't have meant what he said, wasn't thinking straight himself. His eyes were bloodshot, strained from his hours of overtime, living his days in a cloud of mortar dust. No wonder he forgot himself. "I'll put a stop to this," she muttered, circling the car with her hands on her hips, figuring she was about as impressive as a houseboat down on the bay turning itself. Let some smart-ass call names to her face. If folks wouldn't stand up and be counted, before long the only ones left would be college graduates, women who had lost their men, nothing in the lot but foreign jobs that wouldn't begin to hold anybody well grown.

Big Jim brought her back, snapping her on the seat of her pants with the washrag. "Get a move on." She yelped and he shrugged, grinning. "She don't do that bad. Ten, twelve around town. Better on the road." He picked up the hose, insult and indignity streaming away in the water collecting at the curb, his face softening. Irene recalled the gigantic mulberry tree which had once stood in front of the house overhanging their parking place—stopping up the storm drains with its roots, dropping berries. One day one too many overripe berries hit the roof of the polished car, and just like that Big Jim had the tree cut to the ground and hauled off. On her way to the house to fix him a Coke, Irene made a pass, giving him more than a soft elbow. He sprayed her good as she ran laughing up the steps.

Anna passed back and forth to Jessie's all the next week, but she seemed to have forgotten Irene, never glancing her way. It was a further relief to Irene, because Anna had outdone herself, now wearing a winter overcoat buttoned to the chin, with a ratty fur collar practically pea green. In Jessie's opinion, Anna would never have bothered with Irene's car, but she admitted she got afraid sometimes. One whole afternoon Anna sat on the couch, mumbling about her sex life and drinking crème de menthe, until Jessie finally called a halt and said she had to fix supper. It was after that when she decided to call Anna's husband.

"I might have saved my breath, but I thought he ought to know I was worried, so I told him. He didn't get smart right off, but when I said something about her wearing that fur coat he says, 'I think it does something for her,' laughing like he's as crazy as she is. I went on and hung up the phone." Irene thought he'd laugh out of the other side of his mouth if he knew Jessie knew he didn't last but a second. She could hardly recall the last time she and Jessie had had time to themselves, without some nuisance, and wished Jessie would snap out of it and run her mouth about something worthwhile, like Jim-bo's future or the latest report on her mother-in-law's gallstones.

By Friday Irene had spent so much time out front patrolling the Bonneville, she was thinking maybe they ought to pick up stakes and move on, even if it did look as if they'd been run off. The car deserved a garage with doors that slipped up and down like "Open Sesame." Once before, they'd looked at a place in a tract development, but the woman who showed them around had been stuck-up—acting like she lived there and they were Chinese. Irene had never seen so many windows, extra rooms, and shiny mirrors. When suddenly she came upon herself in one, full-length, the jolt wasn't purely personal, although she was nearly twice as big as she'd expected.

All their stuff could have fit in the pantry, and arranged in the large windowed living room, every last broken spring or worn spot would have taken front center. It was okay for where they were, Freddy wiggling incessantly, racing his cars into the last crook and cranny, so that once she'd found one in her house slipper. But in a new place—Freddy wouldn't even be there, an unimaginable thought. Irene boiled, remembering the real-estate lady's pursed lips when Big Jim said he was a stone mason, as though their money wasn't good enough. Next time he could call himself a contractor for Mrs. Rich Bitch.

"Don't y'all fret about your car, lady," Jessie said out her kitchen window, as if she'd been reading Irene's mind. "It's still the best sight we've got in a country mile." Living next to Jessie sure did make a house a home, another reason for staying put, and Irene fixed herself comfortably on the stoop with instant iced tea and her wide-brimmed hat, observing company arrive for the draft evader. Probably they were working themselves into a lather over the march next day in D.C., hoping to get arrested so they could declare an orgy. Peas in a pod, all of them without real work—standing, marching, sitting, all one and the same.

No boy could keep long hair right, letting it mat and frizzle, sizzling in the sun like grass fires. Sometimes there was that same sweet smell in the air around them. Usually they left together in a sorry car they'd trifled with, painted with posies, suns, and rainbows. It was a circus act to see that many narrow behinds, all in blue denim, vanish into something the size of a spittoon. They could pretend they didn't know she was alive, but she'd caught them slipping her the once-over, half embarrassed, like making petty withdrawals at a savings bank. Not one would have known how to manage a sizable balance.

Jessie came out and slam-banged a bucket of dirty water into the weeds beyond the fence. Their houses were lined up like a row of family headstones before the rectangular plots of crabgrass, as if all of them had kicked the bucket from heart disease and didn't know it. Irene had Heart Fund on the brain, the little box now abandoned to the upstairs bureau. If she'd been the woman in charge, she'd have checked up by now, sent the sheriff.

"I might could call her doctor, Irene Lee." Jessie gave her a probing look, like it was a question—Anna on her brain. "I might could tell her to drop dead," Irene thought to say but didn't, looking off so Jessie might figure it out—that she, for one, hadn't the slightest interest. It seemed to her that Jessie's brown eyes looked beady, as if she'd destroy her beauty dogging somebody else's troubles. When there were plenty a lot closer to home.

"Doctors only care if you pay," Irene muttered, too irked to hide it entirely. Jessie dropped her eyes and went inside, letting the door bang hard behind her. "Serves her right," Irene fumed.

Momentarily, she wanted to take it back. Later she'd mix up a batch of no-bake cookies to take over for a peace offering. If she knew Jessie, she couldn't stay mad for long—her boys an example of that. Then Irene remembered the sack of clothes she'd prepared for them, things that had belonged to Jim-bo. They could have gone to Freddy, but Doreen wouldn't have him wear anything that wasn't brand-new, as if new clothes could make up for wholesale neglect. Jessie couldn't be so particular, considering the mortifying condition of her furniture, the charity of the mother-in-law. It seemed impossible Jim-bo had ever worn the batiste nightgown with the embroidered bluebirds that was folded on top of the pile. Irene set it down by Jessie's door, slipping in a handful of peppermints, returning quickly to her own house so she didn't have to see it plopped there like a baby left on a doorstep.

About seven o'clock, Doreen drove into the lot, late from buying out the stores. "Jesus, I'm horny," she called to Irene, as if the whole world cared. She was in a hurry, trying to sneak inside and make it with the sack artist before Freddy got wise. Sometimes in the mornings, Doreen called up, giggling about the double thrill of two men in bed, one of them supposed to be Freddy. Irene wanted to hang up, but she figured that kind of thing went with a paycheck. In another mood, Doreen would call, crying her eyes out, swearing she was leaving the son of a bitch. Right then Freddy rose up, pale, out of the twilight, his throat gulping with excitement. Irene could search for hours but his mother's arrival conjured him in an instant.

"Didja bring me somethin?" he trilled, helping Doreen tote a shopping bag to the house, no second glance for Irene.

"Now, you be good for Daddy so's you won't get a licking," she hushed him. That man no more his daddy than the man-in-the-moon.

"I been waiting all day," he whined, making all day sound like all year, hopping from foot to foot. What was the matter with him? Irene took good care of him, letting him go off and play with the others, buying him little trinkets at the dimestore. She'd have to settle his wagon before he sweet-talked her right out of a job. Doreen had on a new print dress, the second that week, although she already owed Irene from the week before. It didn't sit right with Irene. In the two years she'd been watching Freddy, Doreen had never so much as given her a handkerchief,

scarcely a kind word. Besides, Doreen, arrayed like the lilies of
the field, was still built like a hank of sisal hemp. Cross as Irene
felt, she was glad for the end of the week, and when Freddy
went in his house, pretty soon she heard the old man snarl, then
some thumps and bumps. He'd be a nervous wreck the next day,
poor thing. Doreen could have him!

It was just after dark when Bud Wheeler dropped off Big Jim,
laying rubber, spinning gravel. He was a has-been heller with
fallen arches, but they were all in the same boat and Irene gave
a rebel yell, "See ya tomorrow," flying in the face of the rest of
them who were afraid to speak above a whisper.

She hadn't fixed any supper yet, the kids out until late, and
on a Friday night Irene never knew just when Big Jim would be
home since he'd taken to stopping off at Moony's for a beer.
Sometimes he wasn't a bit hungry. The once she said something,
he'd narrowed his eyes. Said it relaxed him to stay out, nothing
to worry about. She didn't bother to remind him that it was him
coming home that relaxed her, but she showed it, nestling into
him, comfortable. Smooching his cheek and neck, taking liberties
with his hand, trying to coax it to life against her front. It just
lay there, until he withdrew to strike a match for his cigarette,
and then he didn't move back.

Smoking had never appealed to Irene, and when Big Jim first
knew her he swore she put the flowers to shame. He aimed to
burrow himself, eat her with a spoon like fresh cream. Cream it
was—her daddy called her "sweet thang," handing her extra
change on the sly so she'd have a new ribbon for school, a box
for her pencils. When he came in from work, sometimes she'd
lean up against his leg while he rubbed her back; behind them
in the rocker her mamma's pause, the stifled silence. They called
from the factory to tell the family. Her daddy was already dead,
he'd gone so quick. Irene didn't sleep even that one night in the
house and directly after the funeral she left town. Mamma had
the four boys, but there wasn't anything left for Irene.

Big Jim was looking at her queerly and she heard her lungs

laboring like they needed a bail-out. A man like Big Jim, who'd come home to her every night of their life together except when he was in the war, needing and deserving everything she had to give. "I'm saving my babysitting money, Jimmy." She drew herself up, sure with her resolve.

"Don't go and spend it all to one place." He chuckled and reached around to deliver her a snappy-Jo, cheering her so she went on to ask about what she'd been pondering. "What'd you s'pose it takes to go to college?"

"What's that, baby. Y'all aiming to get yourself an education?"

"Not hardly. Just thinking. About Jim-bo, his future and all." It did sound half-baked when she said it out loud, same as before.

"Yeah. And Betty Marie can go to astronaut school while you're at it. Shit, Irene Lee." In the half-light, Irene saw the muscles in his jaw protruding like bunions. He shot his cigarette into the dark and went inside.

She wasn't going to burden him with what her days were like, on guard over their few possessions, sitting on top of Division Hill, her youth gone, neighbors at every hand spoiling for a fight. It *was* pretty farfetched, particularly if you reckoned the times the truant officer called for Jim-bo. She didn't blame Big Jim. One thing for sure, no man would ever have to take nagging and fault-finding from Irene. Her daddy had like to killed himself working the most part of seven days a week, to get some peace and quiet. Got religion too, allowing Pastor Clump to immerse him at the temple, going with Mamma to regular services. Once, he'd asked Irene if she'd come along. She'd noticed then his color was off, but she'd answered sharp anyway. By then she was engaged to Big Jim and didn't need to look to anybody else.

Big Jim lay on the couch with a beer, watching television, when Irene went in the house. She set bread and bologna, mustard, and some cold roasting ears out to eat. There wasn't time to cook up the hamburger she'd defrosted. The next day she'd bake a meat loaf, early, before the afternoon heated up. From the television she heard bursts of gunfire, and some special reporter was there, beside himself in Vietnam. Then some colored folks started complaining. The channel flipped to colored people laughing their heads off, and Big Jim groaned, padding his way to the table, a man so large he could hardly squeeze his thighs underneath, and sat with his chair pushed back. Irene sat across from him, arms in a heap where her plate should have been. She wouldn't eat just then, for she'd been gaining weight and that afternoon had killed her appetite with candy. Later, when Big Jim went on, she'd have a bite.

Big Jim ate in a hurry, like he hardly knew what he was doing, then lit a cigarette, striking the match one-handed, something slick he used to do when they lay in bed after making love, hugging each other longer than it would take to smoke a pack. He got right up, looking kind of baffled to see her there. "I'm right tired." He grinned, seeming to explain, going over to the couch. Before long he was asleep, and she put the food away, piecing on the last of the corn. Commotion from different televisions came in the window beside her, kids laughed or fussed, the chow from two doors down barked frantically—in that neighborhood even dogs had to hold a foreign pedigree. Then one by one, as though there'd been an alarm, doors and windows slammed, in September the nights cooling swiftly as the day's heat evaporated in the high thin air of autumn. Irene felt almost peaceful, dozing over the dishpan, as though her mood could lift as readily and float away. Big Jim slumbering close at hand, his mouth partly open. Tomorrow they'd clean and wax the car, drive to Bowie for the races, and afterward go somewhere and dance. When Hayward McQuig took his turn with her, she'd let him have a good shaa-boom, twirl him under Big Jim's nose. He knew she'd never look at anybody else, but he wasn't a dead man yet. Maybe Jessie would fix her hair, a six-inch bouffant, transparent as a halo in the neon. That is, if she and Jessie were still speaking.

The phone rang, quarter after ten. Either an emergency or the

one somebody she knew who would be that rude. Big Jim, startled
and rubbing his eyes, picked up his shoes and took a beer to the
porch while Irene went to the phone. She cut the light to make
it more peaceful, turned up the fan. It wouldn't ever occur to a
man that something could be wrong. Later she'd fix him popcorn
drenched in butter, have some herself.

When Irene hung up, she went out to join Big Jim, surprised
to find the porch was deserted. Ordinarily, she might have sung
out for him, but the neighborhood seemed remote, everything
familiar set ajar, the parking lot littered with cars, abandoned
like boulders after an avalanche. The mostly shattered street
lamps appeared to hover like the prehistoric monsters Freddy
played with, brought back big as life.

Voices reached her then, from the house across the way where
the divorcée lived with her little girl, and a man and woman
came out. It was no wonder Irene failed to recognize Big Jim
immediately, in company with a complete stranger, a woman
who'd looked a hole through her since she'd moved in—in cahoots with the draft evader. She was young, not much more than
a girl, with long, slim legs, hair to the waist hanging with the
set of an ironed drapery.

Their two shadows dipped and swayed, fell into each other's
arms in the light of the lantern the girl swung as they strolled
toward her car, Big Jim carrying a large toolbox. At the car he
fell on his knees and disappeared. While he was underneath, the
girl held the lantern over her head or lowered it, every now and
then rooting in the box and handing him something. Irene heard
Big Jim's low chuckle or sometimes a light curse, a lilt to his
voice she hadn't heard for a long time. The girl answered as if
they had already been intimate, in fragments, throaty and terrible. Irene lowered herself to the stoop, although until then it
hadn't occurred to her she was standing, waiting the whole endless time Big Jim was busy with the car, the light of the lantern
swinging crazily, shooting beams like things crashing in the sky,

the low hoarse murmuring and scuffles gathering into a coun-
terweight as though her heart had collapsed within her.

Then he was coming back to her, whistling tunelessly, every
step making something real of the night, a bridge projecting
across a canyon. The girl called, "Hey, man, thanks," a cas-
ualness that alarmed Irene more than if she'd bared her breasts.
She could just imagine her in college, learning how to cuss and
talk dirty, how to keep herself thin.

"Poor thang," Big Jim said, speaking like his young self still.
"Wasn't getting nowheres by herself. They got a big day tomorrow, she says. Some kinda march." There was no measuring
the degree of satisfaction underlying his words. The two of them
had first met over a carburetor, and before it went any further
but knowing what would happen next, they'd buzzed every
hangout in three towns, announcing their intentions on two
wheels, drinking fast before they fled on. Last, they'd gone to
the colored dive near the flour mill where Big Jim could drink
when his friend T was tending bar. Irene hadn't been down there
since the night the old woman took her somewhere, a hat yanked
down over her eyes—after Irene handed over the money. She'd
found it on the ledge, in the place where the cream usually was.
Her daddy must have heard her, sick to death every morning in
the outhouse. The trip with Big Jim to the other side of town
marked like a death the division between her life as a girl and
the woman she would be for him. Just then, a light switching
on across from them, in the bedroom of the girl with the car,
seemed as drastic, given the quick self-forgetful way Big Jim
flung up his head.

"Doreen was on the phone just now. She's got to go in tomorrow. Wants me to take Freddy. I told her you might not like
it, it being Saturday and all."

"All right," he breathed, gazing across like a moonstruck calf.
"We can use the money," she managed to say, and got up to
call Doreen back. He might scoff at her babysitting, but it would

add up. To what she couldn't imagine right then, venturing into the dark living room with the moonlight shining through the trees out back, the little scrap of woodland remaining since the model community had expanded with single-family units. It filled the room in the netted shadows and canyons of an eerie future. She turned on the overhead light.

Big Jim waited by the stairs until she hung up, his work boots in hand going up to the closet for their weekend rest. "I got to take the car over to Hank's anyways. Put her on the lift. Something's funny about them shocks." He hesitated, but Irene shrank from meeting his eyes and he went on. Overhead she heard the pad of his feet, the creaking floorboards. She wondered if he was standing then, in the dark of the room, looking across to the other window. One curtain was riding out in the breeze, the light switched off for the night. In the misty pallor of the moonlight, the Bonneville appeared to draw nearer and withdraw, in rhythm with the curtain, midnight blue, as if a severed root of the bygone mulberry tree had taken hold, reaching up from the dirt below.

In the morning a sheet of paper was stuck in the door handle. Irene let it sail away after a glimpse of the word "march." She stood in the shadow of the house, watching the draft evader and two wire-haired boys walk to the car Big Jim had so freehandedly fixed for them the night before. She recognized his touch in the purr of the motor. When the girl came up last, carrying a batch of papers, she took her place in the driver's seat. By the light of day her hair was a steady transparent sheet, as though it had been clear-starched. Anybody could see she aimed to have herself a time, off with three jailbirds. Free as a bird herself, all she needed was some of those birth-control pills. Nothing like being fifteen at the flour mill—no use crying over spilt milk. As the carful of young people passed by, the four of them held up two fingers, grinning at Irene. A sign for something like bullshit.

Irene loomed over the breakfast table, thighs heavy into the Formica, pouring coffee into cups, handing out buttered toast.

Jim-bo and Betty Marie sat there with Big Jim, half asleep but home at last. Irene's body felt quivery as a milk pudding, after only fitful sleep, but Big Jim was himself, scrubbed shiny, his wet sandy curls nested like brown eggs. "We'll go tonight?" To herself it sounded as though she was begging, the hand with the coffeepot trembling.

"We ain't never missed once. Have us a ring-jangled time." He grabbed her onto his lap, squeezing, the sunburnt lines folded around his eyes in secret fans. But soon he moaned that she was enough to cut off the breath of life, and she hurried up before the smile slid off his buttery lips, his eyes golden too in the glint of the Formica. The children rested sourly on their elbows, resentful at any adult fooling, their bent heads duplicates of Big Jim's. The way hers was before age darkened it. Maybe Jessie could brighten her with a bottle of something, put in some henna highlights.

"I purely do not feel like putting up with Mr. Brat today," Irene declared, watching Freddy wander along the walk, slowing down the closer he got, staring back at his mother's car pulling away. If the child was more on the sunny side, he'd get on better. But then he couldn't help that—there wasn't a whole lot to rejoice over where he came from. She put a smile on her face and waved out the window.

"Give the kid a break, Irene Lee," Big Jim rebuked her, not seeing her smile, and she blushed with her back still turned. As if she wouldn't treat a child decent. Big Jim reached out to poke Freddy in the middle as he passed the table, but Freddy flinched, ducking his way farther into the room before he grinned back, limp and shaking. Too much excitement or fear, too much of something. Big Jim shrugged, his large face bland as he forgot Freddy and told the kids to be ready in five minutes if they expected to ride with him. Jim-bo was welcome to go along to the garage and he'd drop Betty Marie at the dairy store. "Five minutes." He took a screwdriver out to the car.

Freddy approached the table and stood eyeing the kids, his tow-colored hair shaved to the bone, giving him a wasted look as though at his age he'd turned gray. He carried a queer-looking G.I. doll which Irene thought was about the kind of soldier most draft dodgers would have made. Jim-bo showed his first signs of life, grabbing the doll and hiding it so Freddy began to whine and giggle at the same time in his overwrought fashion. Irene ordered Jim-bo to cut it out and he let her take the doll after a couple of spars. Why she'd ever imagined he'd settle down in school was beyond her. What he needed was some marching orders. Irene settled Freddy on the couch with his bib on, warning him to stop wiggling so he didn't smear butter on the upholstery.

"Mamma, he's . . ." Betty Marie shrieked, kicking at her brother with her heeled shoe, and he laughed evilly when she stubbed her toe against his shin. Irene hadn't ever been as thin and dainty-looking as Betty Marie, getting her own figure before she knew how to manage it.

"You don't care," Betty Marie accused Irene from across the room, wiping at tears while Jim-bo pulled the horrible faces of an untold agony, a contortion that halted when Big Jim blew the horn from outside.

Betty Marie sprang out of the house, vowing to tell her father, her stylish skirt riding up over her long legs as she slid in beside Big Jim and locked the door. He turned up the radio, winking at Betty Marie, who jumped around locking the other doors before she blew her father a kiss. Jim-bo rose from his chair; a salute for Freddy, Irene getting the benefit of a bob of his muscle as he lowered his arm, sauntering out to the car, Big Jim leaning massively on the horn. The door opened to his touch, Big Jim done with any nonsense, and they were off. Impossible to believe it was sons, children, that went to war. Before their lives had scarcely begun.

"Kin I wash the dishes, kin I wash the dishes?" Freddy brought her back. There was still a house to keep, a child to mind. She set him on a chair at the sink, tied in an apron to save his clothes. Heaven help him if he went home mussed up or dirty, the old man death on a child having any kind of a good time. She kept her eye out to be sure Freddy was careful too, her dish pattern one she'd picked out and bought for herself after she was married, something she'd seen in a woman's magazine you could buy with the coupons in a sack of flour. If Freddy felt ornery, he was liable to drop one on purpose, but he seemed content, blowing suds over the plates. Next she'd get him a bubble pipe at the dimestore. When she sent him out to play he reached up unexpectedly and hugged Irene. Big Jim ought to have been there for that. She'd found a wooden sword that had once belonged to Jim-bo and handed it to Freddy. "Now, don't go stabbing nobody!" As he carried it down the walk, he appeared almost enfeebled by awe. "Freddy," she said, but he didn't hear and she let him go. She didn't know what she wanted anyway.

Later, when Irene went out to sit on the stoop, there was a plate of fudge on the milk box and a note from Jessie thanking her for the clothes. Then Jessie came out and thanked her in person and Irene thanked Jessie for the fudge and for thanking her and everything was ironed out smooth as silk. She and Jessie seemed close as relatives who couldn't ever stay mad.

"Y'all taking the day off?" Jessie asked, seeing the car was gone.

"Why, honey, what I'm doing today takes sitting." They laughed together, because there was never a day off for them, not as long as anything needed doing—including the ironing in the basket, the Heart Fund on the bureau.

Jessie spotted trouble of her own when she leaned to peel a rose off the side trellis and spied her husband's car parked halfway into the field adjoining their yard. She didn't have to say anything, her circumstances marked on her face like dark writing. She went into her house and returned with the car keys, the rose stuck in her buttonhole. Irene thought it would have taken

more than a rose with the Spaniard up in her bed. She figured
to wait to ask about a hairdo.

The community exterminator put in a visit before noontime,
going into the end house on her row, his metal tank and lengths
of tubing hanging off him like tackle. The sum total of his efforts
was to drive the cockroaches toward the other end, until they'd
get so thick and bothersome he'd be called to route them in the
other direction. Irene was proud they pretty much passed her
by. She was that careful to put food away and washed out her
cupboards with Lysol every month.

Freddy sat in the neighbor's sandbox, his stomach bare as
usual, one of Doreen's bargains short of the mark. He was busy
emptying cup after cup of sand out of the box onto the ground.
It was store-bought, white and purified against pinworms. Sideways, he watched the mother at the clothesline, while Dale, the
sand's rightful owner, beside him under the peppermint-striped
canopy, turned red in slow motion, frozen in grief as he watched
his lovely sand disappear in the grass. Freddy poured faster,
shaking his leg to a blur. Until finally, tears broke down Dale's
cheeks and he found voice, howling, bringing his mother on the
run. All innocence, Freddy was as quick, scooping sand back
the other way, shrugging his shoulders spasmodically.

Dale's mother was the soul of patience, so Irene didn't feel
like such a poke, just sitting, watching the show. Freddy was
told to go home, she and Dale had to go downtown. In her native
Texan she squealed for Dale to get in the car. If Irene ever voted,
that accent alone would have kept Lyndon Baines riding a horse.
Her first vote might go to that cocky little son-of-a-bitch from
Alabama—see what her neighbors made of that. Though, truth
to tell, neither of them was worth a damn. Freddy slunk off
somewhere, and mother and child walked to the car carrying a
mix of signs with letters big enough so Irene could read them:
END, HO, STOP. Dale tottered along with one. MAKE LOVE NOT WAR.
Wasn't that something to expose a child to.

The empty surface of the asphalt swam in waves of heat. No one came or went. A blackbird sat stone still in a crabapple tree. He might have been ornamental, with a pasted eye. Mr. Wink stepped out to spit. "I could lick the world," Irene called, companionable. He lingered a minute, blinking, then went inside. Irene felt ornamental herself, propped before her doorway with the sun hat overhanging her like an upset birdbath, watching the world go by.

When the air-raid siren went off, over on the corner, Irene felt a life-rush of fear and flight, two emotions that had her jumping up with the kind of pep she hoped she'd show in the event of a real emergency. Her heart still flip-flopped when she settled back again, reminding herself that it was one of the monthly tests and not the end of the world. In the near-distance a chorus of dogs howled and several terrified youngsters hightailed it for home, screaming bloody murder. There was no need for that, Irene thought, gripping the rotating steel trumpet with a glare of hate, the government scaring them to death. Knowing if ever there was an attack, she'd be the last to know, stranded on a hill in broad daylight, trying to tell herself it was nothing.

Across from Irene the procession wound on the central grass a few seconds before she came to and realized that it was for real. A wavery line of different-sized children followed behind a woman, all of them moving their mouths, although nothing could be heard over the roar of the siren. It was Anna at their head, robed in a long white gown, like a nightdress. The children wore white too and masks, painted in gaudy colors, shaped into the heads and crests of giant birds. Some carried rakes or other tools, using them like staffs, and poles with scraps of white hanging off them. Irene caught the glint of knives and polished steel, which threw more light than the lighted candles amid them. High up, Anna held a flaming torch as she floated over the grass, her hair let loose, moving relentlessly, as though she was propelled forward at the prow of a fast-moving ship. Moving straight toward Irene. A couple of children tripped, then picked up and went on, gathering up dragging skirts. The candlewicks held a static fire, unattached, as though they had been shocked out of the heat.

It felt that same way to Irene when she recognized Freddy among the children, jabbing the wooden sword into the ground in his unmistakable mechanical fashion. Her shock leveraged her into forward action and she lunged off the porch as if trap-sprung, crossed the intervening lot, accomplishing her mission and returning before she half thought about it. Dragging and jerking Freddy by the arm, half toting him, she was spent and breathless when she met Jessie at the junction of their fences, her baby clinging to her hip as she gained speed toward the lot.

"Good God, Irene Lee. She's got more children over there. You want somebody to burn up?" and she ran on, her back seeming to bear the ugly wooden expression Irene had read in her eyes. The siren had wound to a halt without her even noticing it.

Irene braced herself, staggering into the leafy gloom of her house, the spinning ripple of the fan. She let Freddy drop, leaning on the wall with a yank at the venetian shade. He crept away and went upstairs on tiptoe. Irene felt too shaken to fix his lunch, even the soup cold from the can that Doreen told her to give him. Jessie's accusation had taken up in her head where the siren left off, her words different but as cold, like her mamma, who had mocked her for being her daddy's girl. She'd find out what men were like. Her time would come. Irene remembered when she'd bought herself a Lana Turner sweater and went to model for her mamma. How her mamma turned away as if it was sickening.

Another siren started up, this one mild compared to the air-raid warning. Irene lifted a slat, careful so Jessie wouldn't see. An ambulance came in the lot, pulling up beside the few women who stood around where Anna sat on the grass, her torch held up as though it was still flaming, her eyes staring hard at nothing. Most of the children had gone. Jessie's hair was rolled up in fat pink-brush curlers, Saturday-style, ballooned out to the sides like a hat the Pope would wear—an old joke that wasn't funny to begin with. Probably now Jessie would take it for an insult.

Jessie helped Anna and her boy into the ambulance then; handing her baby to one of the mothers, she got in too. As they moved off, the siren wailed again, leaving Jessie's baby screaming behind. The quiet of naptime descended on the neighborhood as they all went indoors, but Irene felt the same urge as the baby, as if she belonged in a lunatic asylum and would run after Jessie calling, "Take me." The canna lilies in Mrs. Wink's garden marched in silence like the dead, bearing orange plumes through a forsaken world. Irene felt it like a horror, her brow caked with a cold moisture. Slowly, she climbed the stairs into the greater heat, her thighs chafing.

The front room where she and Big Jim slept was an oven under the double front windows, their blond Hollywood bed shimmering like a mirage. The back room was darker, with more air stirring because of the trees. It was Betty Marie's alone, now that she was grown, Jim-bo sleeping down on the living-room Hide-a-Bed. Irene had fixed it up like a dream room with its canopy and a matching flowery spread and curtains. Freddy took his naps in there and Irene lay down beside the slumbering child, closing her eyes and taking sleep like a drug she'd craved a long time.

When she woke, at first she didn't know where she was, still struggling in her dream, panting, her heart rent. Her mamma had been holding her while Irene tried to tell her, begging, but she wouldn't listen, forcing Irene down into the dirt, like an open grave. Awake, Irene could still smell the drying medicine her mamma used on the eczema that had withered and aged her skin from a young age. Lying with her eyes closed, she could count on her own hands and arms the rash of burns that came from ironing—before one healed, another took its place. Eyes opened then, the crumpled sheet Freddy had worn, dropped to the floor along with the wooden sword, brought back the parade, and she turned toward Freddy, catching a flash as his eye closed, quick as a minnow.

She saw the blood then, crusted around his nose and mouth, more smeary on his cheek, the smell from the dream. There were stains on the pillowsheet, his clothes, some on her arm where he'd touched her. Freddy's lashes quivered fretfully against his cheek, although he didn't move, even as a fresh red line crawled toward his mouth under the hollow of his nostril.

Irene hauled up off the bed without speaking, and bringing a damp washcloth from the bathroom, she washed Freddy's face and hands while he continued faking, as if she was some sort of a dummy too. When she was done she went in the other room for the matches on the bureau.

She'd been there when Doreen had warned Freddy, told him what was going to happen if he ever again made that kind of a mess, blood all over the place. He had to stop fiddling with his nose and making it bleed. Just never touch it, even if it itched something terrible. And if it did happen, he was to call somebody to help him and not try to stop it himself. She didn't like to scare him but, she whispered to Irene, she was afraid Leroy would kill him the next time, he'd beaten him so bad.

For once Doreen had sounded sensible, teaching Freddy in a serious tone while he stared with his snow-colored eyes, nodding as if he understood when she mentioned irritated tissues and those who would help him if he called. Last, she lit a match and made him hold out his fingers, repeating the threat before she blew it out. He cried then, sobbing that he'd be good. He wouldn't do it again. How he got afraid of the blood that wouldn't quit. Irene left the room then. The noises Freddy made when he cried always got to her. Long before they met up, he'd learned to cry that way, as if he was smothering himself.

She was the one responsible, the one who took care of him. She reached to take the matches, but her hand trembled and knocked against the box for the Heart Fund, upsetting it onto the floor, coins clashing and jangling together. A single dime rolled free, blurry like a quick silver hoop. As she bent down to snare it, the dime spun away, and on her hands and knees she started for it just as Freddy rounded the corner and snatched it up. With a gasp of success, he held out the dime on the flat of his hand. "Here, I'ene Lee," his eyes grave and shining, as if, though of uncertain value, it might possibly be the full exchange for a life.

Black Ice

OHAN CALLED JENNY after it was all over and he was already driving his new car. He told her that, as he had become actually airborne, his former late-model Oldsmobile sedan leaving the road at the final curve before the bottom of the hill, after it had glanced off two stranded cars, still with sufficient momentum to lift up and sail one hundred and fifty feet through the ravine, mired at last in a creek bed, he had begun to scream, "I'm going to die. I'm going to die"—more bewildered astonishment in that cry than any terror he could feel. Although there was that too, no doubt about it, and not long afterward he had another of his severe shaking fits. The woman who had stopped for the accident and then offered to drive him home in her car saw the shaking when it began, heard his accelerated breathing, as though he were being activated by a force pump. She pulled off on the side of the road and touched his head gently with her hands. "I was expecting some Feldenkreis massage, but she began, 'Jesus, heal this man. Thou who hast saved him from the horns of death and led him to stand under the myrtle tree.' "

Jenny's fingers stiffened as though still tangled in his dark and curling hair. "Myrtle trees. In Vermont! I haven't been gone that long." She knew she was missing the point, but it wasn't the first time a backwoods Holy Roller had prayed over that lost lamb, strayed from the Eastern Fold.

"She was perfectly serious, Jenny. As a matter of fact, it felt kind of right too after what I'd been through. Like a benediction." Ohan, the apostate, a man dazed and amazed abroad upon the face of the earth, that sublime achievement: a man alive. Jenny accepted his rebuke: since she had moved away and was not with him in his hour of need, it was fortunate that someone was. Let him take comfort where he could.

In spite of the thousand miles between them and their marital separation of six months, Jenny was almost sorry she hadn't been there to make the plunge along with him. She had made so many others. Always they had been together, two children playing day after day, side by side, without touching, like those lines described by Euclid, projecting forever parallel. It seemed that the roadside priestess could have pronounced for each of them. " 'Is it nothing to you, all you who pass by? Look and see if there is any sorrow like my sorrow.' "

The accident came as no real surprise to Jenny. She might have predicted that one day he would take wing, a raven-haired daredevil. His voice was raucous in outcry, while his beaked nose pecked at every disturbance, as though to further aggravate continual misfortune. Bitterness had whittled away at his once full-lipped mouth.

Even as a kid, Ohan had been labeled accident-prone. On an earlier flight, at fourteen, he had escaped old man Snyder, who had caught the four boys on top of his garage where they perched, the better to see the daughter of the house undress in a bowl of light. He broke his nose, the second of three times, in his plummet down the drain spout. But he considered himself lucky, since the Snyder dog had taken a gigantic hunk out of Mikey Menendian's leg. Twice Ohan broke his left arm, and although sleeping sickness is no accident, his family just shook their heads sadly over the aptness of his nickname, Oh-oh.

Much later, as a man, he had rescued a frightened child at the top of a slide, taking her down on his lap. His feet extended flat out before him, he sped like a whiz on the just-waxed surface, hitting the ground with a smack and cracking a dorsal vertebra. Soon though, he was up and walking, propped upright in the steel-staved corset he still wore on weekends and holidays, his back never quite the same.

"You sure were lucky this time," Jenny whispered on the phone, mourning the end of the Oldsmobile, the family car.

"I'll say. More than lucky. Saved is more like it. You know that bend on the Republic Road where they paved the hill? Treacherous."

Jenny knew the place very well. She had first seen their farm-house from there, perhaps fifteen years earlier, long before they had bought it. She had seen it across the intervening ravine, about a mile away if you counted the ups and downs, but plainly visible as the crow flies, surrounded by its orchard and maple trees. It was an unspoiled house, white-frame, hip-roofed, with a widow's walk, true after a hundred years; the only house in sight. A virgin bedecked for the bridegroom, Jenny had thought, seeing it among the tangle of unpruned apple trees blossoming around it.

When she said, "I know just where you mean," she also re-membered their shared contempt when the subject of paving the steep on that dirt road first came up at town meeting and not a voice was raised in dissent, though it didn't take a fortune-teller to know it was better left untouched. Wally Turner did speak up to say he guessed he could stand it, since his house was set a half mile back on his driveway and that meant his kids and dogs weren't likely to wander onto it. Another family had already sold out and moved farther north. The rest of the townspeople voted a prompt, even belligerent "yea," along with the selectmen who had matching funds burning holes in their pockets—all of them disgusted with washboard, washout, potholes, frost heaves, the gamut of back-road Vermont. They were thoroughly sick too of outsiders, urban refugees who thought the struggle with hardship and inconvenience amounted to something more uplifting than men laid up from one mishap or another, women worn out before their time. The natives weren't ashamed to yell out loud and clear for the one thing of value they had, the land and their right to sell it, or improve it. Or spit on it.

Two summers before the paving, the road commissioner had started preparing the Republic Road, engineers and local brawn grading and digging, good pay all around. For four seasons they allowed it to sit, settling and packing. Then in the fall they laid on the asphalt, a slick, leathery coil winding the hill, an improved road, wide enough for a painted dividing line. A sizable portion of the new surface was raised up higher than the old road, and they'd strung guard fences of cord wire along the drop-offs. On the flats they'd left unpaved dirt—until another time.

"Sonofabitch," Ohan yipped on their daily trips over the road, now more than ever a shortcut to the interstate, tossing and slamming from dirt to pavement and back again, stones hailing and chipping the paint on their new car. "Seems like they're just waiting to nail somebody along in here."

That morning when Ohan wrecked the Oldsmobile, a man had been standing out by his car on the side of the road, waving his arms. "I saw him," Ohan admitted. "Couldn't tell what he was trying to say. Or thought I couldn't. But later I knew I did, only it happened too fast, him waving and me already or nearly onto the hill and going down. Black ice. Doesn't show. Just looked like bare asphalt, open road. The second I hit it I knew, the car a toboggan. Freewheeling, going the distance. I was picking up speed—like I wanted it. Even those two cars I hit didn't slow me down. Just boosted me in the turn so that at that last curve I simply took off. Hurtled the rails. Airborne. Until finally I landed, scooting over the ground, somehow missing a forest of trees until I entered Johnny Brook, broke on through the ice, and came to a halt. The whole time I was holding on for dear life, and part of me was thinking, This is an impact-absorbing wheel, the other part screaming that I was dying.

"After I stopped, it took me a few minutes to realize I was living, or that I would even want to be. Wasn't hurt a bit, though, or even messed up. I worked awhile to force the door open and stepped out, picking up my briefcase to carry with me. In case I made it to the office. You should have seen the looks on the faces of those people coming on down through the trees, as if they'd seen a miracle. I only stood to watch them come, the woods all icy and radiant—maybe they thought I was an angel— my feet numb in that running brook where the ice had shattered when the car went through. At least that was ice you could see. Thin ice. I wasn't shaking yet, although it did occur to me, leaning there with my arm on the roof of the car, that I had survived something like a plane crash. The old guy who came up first must have been thinking the same thing. 'Jesus,' he said. 'I never did see a car fly like that, except maybe on the television.' "

Ohan had joined the Air Force Reserve at seventeen, hoping to be a pilot, the same as his older brother, who flew in World War II. There were old snaps of a skinny, suave-looking kid in khaki, in sunshine, his hair slicked back and casual against a palm tree in Florida, Ohan and the palm tree alike in girth and incline. In some pictures he wore one of those long aviator scarves tossed to the four winds. Looking rakish, although he'd been assigned to Intelligence and never got to fly, sitting out the war in Kansas.

"You know, Oh," Jenny said over the phone, a thousand miles away, their voices still traveling side by side though bound in opposite directions. "It reminds me of that accident we had in Charlottesville. Before we got married. We slid on a hill that time too, remember—our first accident." A fondness had crept into her voice with the nickname.

They had been riding in Ohan's Buick, an old clunker, his

first car, coming home from one of his weekly sessions with a hypnotist who was trying to remedy his nearly constant headaches. Right after they'd begun to descend the hill, the police had started setting up a roadblock, but Ohan and Jenny saw that only later, looking back up after the accident. At the time, going down, they stared to the front, aimed down the whitening road with its jagged design of tire tracks fading under the falling snow. No other cars were in sight. Ohan had felt the car lose traction on the downward pitch, and as it evened itself out sideways, he wheeled violently into the direction of the breakaway. Then the other way. Until it was of no particular use to do anything and he'd just stuck his arm out to protect Jenny, as a parent will guard a small child, and they watched themselves wafting and spinning toward the thin saplings edging a ravine. They twirled in suspended weightlessness, then a small tree stopped them short of the embankment. It had been very quiet. They had been quiet, the whole thing entrancing even in the moment of collision there on the edge of the bank, the city in snow silent around them. The car's motor had quieted abruptly too, because with the impact something inside had come loose, something vital, and the entire engine had fallen from its housing and rested beneath them in the snow. The hood ejected and landed in the woods. They had not changed positions except they sat closer together on the slipcovered bench seat, staring out at the gaping hole where once the engine had hung.

"Next you got the Chevy," Jenny urged through the receiver, recalling each car, the order they came in. She had always been nervous about driving. "The kiss of death," her father called Jenny when he gave up teaching her himself and sent her to driver's education. That didn't work either, but Ohan, a young man, came into her life and was the soul of patience, teaching her to drive in the Chevy. "We could see ground underneath us in that one too, through the rust holes. Remember?" Looking down at the speeding land had been a bit like flying low.

"I carried a gallon of oil in the back, fed it like a baby. It had Dynaflow—one of the first. There was a time I could have told you the name and model number of any automobile at forty feet. Now I hate the goddamn things. I'd like to blow every one of them sky-high. Maybe that's what I'm doing, taking them out one at a time. You know, Jenny, the first car I wrecked was an Olds. My dad's. Brand-new. I took it for a spin on Lakeshore Drive, a little joyride on the sly. Ran right up this guy's ass. Seems like I've come full circle."

"Seems to me you got that wish of yours."

"You bet," Ohan said, but he didn't laugh. He had often planned the perfect accident, had it down and recited it to Jenny like a bedtime story. It would reprise every time the current family car had reached that stage when it was worth more dead than alive. The distinguishing feature of the perfect accident was that although the car would be totally demolished no one would be hurt.

"You even said a cliff," Jenny reminded Ohan. She had learned to listen very carefully to everything he said, hoping strict attention might reconcile their differences, mend the widening breach. "You said you'd send it headlong off a cliff."

"A prophet in his own time. Kind of creepy, don't you think? Wish some of my other wishes would come true." There was the trunkful of money that one day Ohan would magically stumble across and the vain hope, persisting since law school, that he would metamorphose into a reading machine. As his insomnia worsened and became chronic, lying beside Jenny through the endless nights, Ohan wished he would go to sleep and never wake up. Insomnia could be contagious, and with increasing frequency Ohan retreated to the back bedroom at night to read or to toss and turn as he might. "I wish you'd get the hell out of here and leave me alone," he'd snarl if Jenny objected, and she wished things would go back to the way they used to be.

"The cliff I had in mind—it wasn't a thing like in Vermont.

No, it was somewhere out West and really stupendous. No fooling around, so that when the car took off it just disappeared into the wild blue yonder. Of course there was never a driver. I never expected to find anyone fool enough for that. I figured I was only the brains behind the operation, the one to explain things to the insurance company."

Ohan was good at that, and insurance companies could be patient too, as though there was a patience parameter in their computers. Everybody knew who got the bill for that—nothing was free. Just the winter before, they had been able to collect on a mysterious, even incredulous, accident to the Plymouth Valiant. Ohan had been out late the night before and when he came home had gone to the back bedroom. Jenny was up at her usual early hour, in the dark, drinking her coffee while staring out the window as dawn made its appearance. Gradually revealing to her wondering eyes the distorted front end of their car, which had been parked far up in the yard near the porch. At first she thought its condition a trick of the light on the new-fallen snow.

She opened the door and stood in the murky gloom of the north bedroom across from the blanketed mound of her husband. When he didn't budge she walked over to the window and snapped the shade to the top so it spun and flapped, and then she raised the window, propping it open with a stick. Still, Ohan didn't twitch on the ancient springs of the bed Jenny and her sister had shared for the years of their childhood. His dark hair on the pillow reminded her of her sister, and when she turned away it seemed that, like her sister, he could be gone any instant, grown up and off to college. But before her loomed the reality of the car, abandoned in the yard. The snow blowing in the window off the metal porch roof netted into the fabric of her nightgown as though she were being cast into a permanent structure. She didn't even shiver.

"Don't you have anything better to do?" It was the tone Ohan

used when she disturbed him in the night, afraid, even his cross-
ness a solid base to touch in the dark.

"The car," she said.

"The car." He struggled to his elbows. "What d'you mean
'the car'?"

Reflecting his dreams and expectations, his eyes met hers,
confirming him as the victim of consciousness, the haunt of
circumstance. He leapt from the bed, all poise, a swordsman. At
the window he was at the ready, stout-hearted, resourceful—she
had seen him employ a host of devices, ski goggles at the bar-
becue pit, a rope secured to the chimney holding him while,
upside down, he replaced roof slates. Once, to spare an innocent
creature suffering, he had driven twice over a wounded opossum.
She used to think her watching mattered to him, but now he
seemed more than ever absolutely alone.

"Well, I'll be damned." He shook his head as if to clear it, as
if now he was ready to join in Jenny's suspicions that he was
probably drinking too much, too steadily. When she walked in
the bedroom she hadn't thought about the smell, but now she
recaptured the soured sweetness amid the sweeping cold with
snow blowing across the floor. Ohan hunched forward, leaning
his hands on the sill, a bather in his shorts and T-shirt, ready
to take the plunge. "How in blazes. I had three fucking beers."

He grabbed his robe and with it unbelted and billowing around
him soared through the hall and took the stairs, the hall below,
the kitchen and porch, to come to rest in front of the car. From
the window, Jenny saw him reappear. She hadn't tried to follow,
couldn't keep up, would break her neck. Ohan studied the
smashed bumper and crumpled fender, then rapidly surveyed
the visible territory of the orchard, woodland, and meadow. He
searched up and down the road for signs of intruders, examined
the porch spindles for any kind of clue. "What do you know
about this?" He glared up at Jenny.

Later Ohan said the thrill was gone, right after he didn't find blood and the police weren't putting on the heat for a hit-and-run. Eventually they pieced together a probable scenario. Ohan remembered a few things: he had left the bar with his friend Arthur. "It sits way the hell up on that bluff, overlooking the river and the interstate. A lot of out-of-state drunks get to admire the view. I remember it did seem a little funny when we came out, as if the car wasn't exactly where I thought I'd left it. But I couldn't decide on what was different, so I just got in and drove home. I did notice a headlight was out."

From there they reasoned backward, deducing that Ohan didn't pull the hand brake after parking in the steep lot. Or didn't pull it hard enough. Somebody must have nudged the car while he was inside, so it coasted forward and settled into the guardrail that protected the underlying highway. The insurance adjuster said it happened all the time; rationality and the logic of circumstances had his confidence. But Ohan wasn't so certain. Perhaps even then he felt events aligning themselves mysteriously according to another obscure and irreversible progression, to culminate in the perfect accident.

"I don't believe it," Ohan had said to Jenny during one of the early phone conversations after their separation. "It's not natural, talking to you like this, all civilized. I ought to be strangling you or hanging myself."

"Life doesn't have to go on like an Italian opera," she started to say, but stopped herself. She was confused too and didn't know what was in either one of them. "We're doing the best we can," she begged lamely for absolution from somewhere. "It just happened."

"But I wasn't paying attention. How did I end up like this? What did I do wrong? What did I agree to?"

Jenny began to remind him that he'd been fed up with her for years, but he interrupted. "Yeah. Me with the uncanny knack for getting what I want. So here I am. A man alone. Living in a nine-room house on ten acres of land. Alone. Could this be what I wanted? One pathetic guy riding around in a Prussian war horse of a car, three or four tons of steel to carry me ten miles and back from work so I can be alone again. Every day there's less of me too, since I'm surviving on bread and water. Gas is over a buck a gallon. I'm a living anachronism. Boy, if I could hire somebody to drive that baby off a cliff—that would solve some headaches. I'd collect the insurance and buy something sensible." Something soothed in his tone then, the relief of being sensible—if only in his wildest dreams. "Too bad I can't pay somebody to smash into it good and hard, destroy the thing."

"You already had that accident," Jenny said. One morning the year before, he'd backed solidly and decisively into their own second car, which had been parked behind the Oldsmobile, big as life. Facing Jenny, who was staring out the kitchen window, Ohan had reversed, plowing into her car, wearing an expression she'd seen before when, at a great clip, he'd pass their house on the dirt road, driving too fast to make the turn into their drive. Or he was oblivious to it perhaps, speeding by, oblivious to his whereabouts, too preoccupied with what he was thinking about or the sheer act of driving, his expression one of savage onslaught, of revenge, escape, steel-gripping the wheel, his hair wind-filled amid the stones and dust spumes that enveloped his passage, the bit in his teeth. She'd watched him pass, alarmed and fascinated. A marked man, a stranger. Jenny would be there to see him, because any car approaching that recklessly on the curving country road brought her to the window, trembling and furious at the danger to the innocent, children, the enfeebled, dogs. She ran to the window to identify the madman. Those times, seeing Ohan, home from the practice of law, she'd felt along with her fury an involuntary release, as though he might indeed be the one with a charmed life, and a few minutes later he would reappear from the other direction, chastened.

"You were flying low," Jenny might comment when he came in the door.

"You know what you can do about it," he answered, if he answered at all.

"You're one hell of a driver," Jenny had sometimes admitted to Ohan, for his driving had rescued them. In San Francisco at an intersection, a car was barreling downhill straight for them and couldn't stop. Ohan had burst forward, flooring the accelerator to save them by inches. Another time the front wheel of their convertible had, at interstate speed, severed completely and Ohan had maneuvered the careening, crippled vehicle to a soft landing. His foot had never once erred to touch the brake and his hands had held to the wheel in the ten o'clock racing position his father had taught him in the days of blowouts and explosive retreads.

"But no amount of steering will help once you're on ice," he reminded Jenny now, after he'd survived the latest accident, after she'd moved away to St. Louis. "You hit it, you're a goner, just taking the ride. And when you don't see it coming, unless the light happens to strike at just the right angle, there's no warning at all, nothing you can do."

Jenny could see the Republic Road again, its gloomy steeps as it wound down from the state forest preserve. Even though it would frighten her, Ohan had sometimes cut the engine to see how far he could get without using the accelerator. Her caution made him angry. He said she didn't trust him. "The light's never good in there," she agreed.

"I tell you, Vermont roads are death on a city boy. I never knew any of this existed. I thought ice was something you skated on at the golf course while the organ played. It was like the sidewalks went on forever, covering the world. I'd see people walk by, people I'd never seen before and would never see again. I figured they were on their way walking around the world."

"When I was a kid," Jenny said, "we used to skate on Lake George. We would go for miles and miles. Seemed it went on forever too. Sometimes that ice would be black. It gets older and thicker and deeper—you'd think it was a glacier. Even though it's black, it's translucent with air bubbles like gems floating deep inside. It's like seeing through ice into the beginning of time. For that to happen it has to stay cold a long time. The snow doesn't have a chance to melt but evaporates right back up into the air."

"Yeah. In chemistry they call that 'sublime. To sublime.' That's exactly how I feel now, up on cloud nine. Happy to be alive. And now that I'm rid of that dinosaur—I couldn't have arranged it any better myself. Couldn't have picked a better car. Good balance, suspension, protection. Your flying Oldsmobile. This little job I have now would have flipped in nothing flat and I'd be wearing a tin can for a halo. I guess I'll have to learn a whole new way of driving, now that I'm back on terra firma."

Jenny wondered where that was, sitting holding the phone after Ohan had said goodbye, listening into the distance until the dial tone interrupted and then a horrible sound commenced. She remembered that when she was a child, a phone off the hook simply went dead. Without Ohan she had to learn a whole new way of living.

She felt dazed, trembling as though she too had made a narrow escape. She might have been with him for that ride, as she'd been with him for so many others. Together they might have gone too far, might have lifted off and flown away. Become sublime, absorbing into the atmosphere, the stratosphere and beyond, to drift in the oldest and blackest, the farthest reaches of endless time.

Aunt Josie

I WAS JUST barely awake in the storm, a little tense, and then in the dance of light over the wall I saw Aunt Josie stepping quickly to lower the window, the great areolas of her breasts two familiar eyes. Aunt Josie slept and conducted all her night-time business in the altogether, the raw, the nude—whatever you want to call it, several different names for the same outfit. Uncle Tim kept on his T-shirt, said his shoulders got cold. I got embarrassed thinking about them together there overhead in the high-backed mahogany bed where they'd been sleeping the eight years of their marriage, Uncle Tim weighing two hundred and fifty, Aunt Josie twenty pounds over her best. That rose in my mind as an awful lot of raw flesh bedding down.

Nights when Uncle Tim was away I'd have the pleasure of sleeping in that bed—Aunt Josie in a worn-through gown she'd retrieved from somewhere, I in my underpants. She'd always check to make certain I'd left them on under my gown, sometimes giving the elastic a snap. "I wouldn't want you to feel insecure," she'd say, and laugh, elbow me in the ribs. But she was a pretty decent bed partner, staying on her own side, with no kicking. I'd slept with a lot of kids and it was pure relief that Aunt Josie didn't have nightmares and sleepwalk, or wet the bed so that I'd be stranded, cold as ice in the dawn, while the kid had the covers and I clutched a sodden sheet, too numb to move.

The summer I was thirteen, I went to stay with Aunt Josie and Uncle Tim, who was the athletic coach at the Evanstown State Farm for boys. Those five hundred boys were always busy, mowing the acres of fields and lawns, tarring the drives, putting up screens, and that was a lot of flesh to think about too. Some of them, maybe all of them, were bad boys, but watching them work took up a lot of my time. They took notice of me too— leaning on their rakes, whistling catcalls if I didn't come near. Aunt Josie had her favorites and they'd find excuses to do things to the huge gray house, which was so broken down excuses came easy, and we served iced tea out the windows, syrup rings puddling the sills, the boys humble and intent, asking if we wanted the porch floor red or tan, and did we like the way they'd shored up the drain spouts with baling wire. Aunt Josie said no house looked right with the appendages sagging, dangling her arms limp to give the effect, allowing that everything they did suited her just fine.

The house was set on a little knoll between some higher hills and, when I came up at it from the street, it looked to me as if it was bobbing in an isolated sea, not even phone lines or electricity attached, things the boys hadn't gotten around to fixing yawing and flapping. They were forever tending the grass, though, so the lawn was watery smooth, stretching and falling green to the distance where the dark file of woods began, beyond which, unseen, was the surrounding iron fence I could mostly forget was there. The phonograph played all day long, and I think of that summer whenever I hear "Sophisticated Lady" or "I Get a Kick out of You." Or whenever I see a house adorned with boys—listing off ladders, lying on the roof slant, sidling around the corner to cop a smoke, music pouring out for everyone to hear.

This night Uncle Tim was gone, traveling around the state, trying to get the legislature to appropriate more money for the sports program he believed would help those boys get some self-respect, have a better chance. As usual Aunt Josie and I were walking to the drugstore on the edge of the Farm where we went in the evenings for Cokes and ice cream, unless there was something special to do, a movie or a baseball game.

"Did you mind that bobwhite singing this evening?" she asked. I could tell she was thinking about the old place, saying "mind" when Mother would have said "notice." "Made me wish I could go on back up home once more." Aunt Josie and my daddy were brother and sister, and they'd been raised up in the high ridge country, where they sometimes ate squirrel meat and parched corn and people said mind when they meant notice. That farm was gone now, or at least belonged to a different family, and I'd only been driven past in the car. But when Aunt Josie talked about it, it was as though I'd lived there too, and I'd see ice skim on washbowls in the early morning, frosty breath and crazy quilts piled high on iron bed frames.

"Aunt Josie," I asked her, walking along. "Did you know Uncle Tim really well when you were married?"

"I thought so at the time. But I guess love isn't much like knowing."

"Then how do you know that you want to live with one man forever, like he's your family? I don't think I'll get married," I added, thinking inside that I'd just like to live with Aunt Josie forever and ever and have the boys come round the house.

"You'll want to get married someday. Have your own family. You'll fall in love." She made it sound like destiny. "You just be real careful you put him in first place, remember he was the one gave you those children." She was thinking back now, voicing an edge of sharpness. "My mamma never could learn that—you don't remember her—but she didn't ever know how to treat a man. She made your granddaddy feel like he was an extra convenience that came with the place, no one important. That just kills the spirit in a man. You pay attention now. Learn how to make a man feel like somebody, like a real special man."

Aunt Josie making Uncle Tim feel like a real special man was another embarrassing thing, because every time he came home after being gone, even just for work, she'd rush over and hang off his neck, kiss him on the mouth, and call him her true love, with the little girls whining and tugging on their legs. I had to go out of the room fast and get busy with something.

Then I asked, "Do you think you should like a boy for how he looks, or how he is on the inside?" She gave me a sidelong, get-serious kind of smile and then I rushed on to what I was really wanting to ask. "Do you think any boy will ever like me, inside or out?"

"I suppose you think those boys come round all the time to see *me*," she said. And of course I did. "Don't you worry, honey. It'll come."

She looked off and I said, hoping, "Nobody likes me." Maybe she'd say more. Maybe there was someone in particular who had noticed me.

"You just make somebody feel special. He'll like that," she said, and then she called up to the girls, "Mary Jane, Nancy," her voice rising and falling in the summer dusk, and the sound was mournful somehow and made me think of my mother and home, the Littleton twins skating up the front walk to see if I could come out. Just then we were passing the deserted-looking brick buildings where the Farm boys slept behind barred windows. Usually we saw them only when they were working outside or playing ball for Uncle Tim. We could almost forget why they were living there, forget they had to be there. We hurried along, looking on down the hill, beyond the gate, to where we could see a few early lights sprinkling over the town. By the time we'd passed through the gate I was glad again to be living there with the five hundred boys mowing the grass and Aunt Josie teaching me how to make a man feel like a real special man.

That was how we talked all summer, after the dishes were washed and we were moving along on the dark asphalt walks in the drifting dusk, swallows arcing the sky, the five hundred boys gone somewhere, their memory suspended in the last golden fall of light across the empty fields, the little girls struggling along behind us, starting to tire from the day. They seemed separate from the two of us; Aunt Josie just waiting for them to grow up enough to think about boys so she could teach them.

At this time of day, Aunt Josie started to look clear alive, as some women do after they've put everybody else first for the whole day while they keep things going. Now she was starting to relax from the inside out, her face easing up. She had put on her white sling backs, the striped cotton dress still hanging with no perceptible shape but looking better, probably because her legs showed up so well in the pumps. Her master stroke was a dot of rouge on each cheek. There was no accounting for the charm of that artifice—it suggested all the bright hopes Aunt Josie had in mind for herself and for me. That's all she did to fix up to go to Bennett's Drugstore, or anywhere else, from what I could tell.

We entered through the side door, directly into the fountain section, the little girls fussing now over a frayed stuffed dog already missing an ear, Aunt Josie scooting them along, naming flavors out loud to get their attention. Ernie stood in his place behind the counter, the apron he wore camouflaged with the spills from summer desserts, his thick, hairy arms teeming with muscles. In their bobbing and jumping they seemed to make an undue display of pulling levers for chocolate syrup or carbonated water. Although he stood quite still when Aunt Josie came into the overheated, close backroom, where the fan spiraled slackly on the ceiling, all of her evening-time pleasure in her face.

"Hey, Ernie," she greeted him, her voice soft and lilting as the mourning doves calling in the dawn back up on the high ridges away from the river.

"Hey, yourself." He leaned forward, smoking steadily, and I

could see his eyes behind his steady grin and the smoke, telling Aunt Josie things that were private, making me look away. "Tim gone again?" I never liked the way he looked at Aunt Josie, the questions he asked. I wondered why she was so nice to him, but then she was nice to every man, making him feel good, making him wish maybe he could be her special man.

Aunt Josie nodded absently and gave me coins to play some music. I picked out two songs, hillbilly, since that was what you could find on a backcountry jukebox. "Tell Cilly to come on out, Ernie." Aunt Josie showed an interest in everyone, but Ernie looked annoyed, tearing himself away from admiring her and yelling over his shoulder for Cilly, who appeared in the kitchen doorway, wiping her hands. A thin, tight-faced woman whose hands at the end of a day doing dishes were as red as if they'd been boiled. She came out with a smile for Aunt Josie, though, and they just clicked along, on the weather, the boys fixing up the house, the trip Uncle Tim was making, until some other people walked in and Cilly vanished back where she'd come from.

"This is my niece." Aunt Josie was introducing me to a woman and her son, a boy from off the Farm who had blond curls all over his head and right away a grin for Aunt Josie that said he wished he could paint her screens and drink her iced tea. The grin spread to me too and I blushed and nodded, my mind empty as a drained pitcher. But Aunt Josie didn't bring people together to abandon them to a stricken silence. She started right in warming up the boy with her jokes, but including me, mentioning my good points by way of conversation. "Of course," she was saying, "when a man is with me he forgets everything. I can't hardly blame him for that. But while you're remarking my beauty, don't forget this girl's fair hair. Though it might strike you as a trifle thick and unruly next to mine." Affectedly, she patted her own wispy hair, soft spun and sparse as the fluff of down scattered alongside a duck pond, her hand making a feathery pretense of primping. She gladly offered up her misfortunes for me. My hair was immortalized after that, and although the boy and I did not talk before he had to leave, Aunt Josie made it seem that we might have.

The evening went along, Aunt Josie asking the boy about his school and the sports he played, telling him that the Farm boys needed uncommon attention, needed to live where they would be treated with respect. She talked to his mother and to me too, pretty much ignoring the two little girls, but everybody was happy with all the joking, Aunt Josie commenting on this and that, though she could listen carefully when other people talked—giving us a taste of a real woman.

Later on, some of the Farm boys came in, perking right up because Aunt Josie was there to call each of them by name and make them feel welcome. One boy, though, took one glance at her and wheeled straight back out the door, pushing two others along with him. That was Taddy Barker, and he took it out on Aunt Josie that Uncle Tim had kicked him off the football team. Partly for gouging and name-calling, but there was more to it, something nobody knew for certain. Aunt Josie confided in me that Uncle Tim blamed Taddy for Millard Potts jumping off the fire escape one winter night, before they had to send him over to the state hospital so he wouldn't destroy himself.

"Hey there, Jamie, Shorty, Frank," Aunt Josie called to them. "Cokes all around and make them doubles." It was a privilege they'd earned, to be allowed out to the soda fountain, and it meant they'd be going home soon. She was telling them and everybody that she knew they were trying to come along and act right, proud of themselves, making her proud too.

"Where's Coach?" Jamie asked, after they'd thanked her for the Cokes, polite as could be.

Aunt Josie didn't answer directly. "He's sure counting on you fellows for Saturday's game. Says you all could whip the pants off those townies if you'd put something more of yourselves into

trying than you did mowing that south quarter. We looked out
for the longest time before we could figure if you were cutting
or weaving daisy chains."

"Jesus, it was hotter'n hell," Shorty said, then blushed and
mumbled, "Excuse me, Mrs. Woods," because, without her saying anything, all those boys wanted to treat Aunt Josie like a
lady. After all, Uncle Tim wasn't one of those coaches who swear
and torment their players, just to show who's tough. Though he
had looks that were fit to kill. Aunt Josie said that it was those
looks that first interested her in Uncle Tim. That was a long time
ago, when they were in school together and he was a running
back for the state university and scared the other team just
staring down the line. She'd never in her life seen more fumbling
and backtracking than at that homecoming game—the away
team never scored. Right then she figured she'd seen a man who
would give a woman something to live up to.

Ernie was trying to get Aunt Josie's attention back on himself,
away from the boys, and he leaned over, confidential. "You want
a touch of extra sweetening in that Coke, Josie?" The blue hula
girl wiggled her hips across his bicep.

But Aunt Josie blurted out, "Thank you, dear, but I don't need
one earthly thing more to make this a perfectly grand evening,"
and we could see that was true in her good-time shining eyes.
She turned again to Jamie Kincaid, who was Uncle Tim's fair-
haired boy, a first-rate pitcher, due to be released from the Farm
after Saturday's game. "I'm hoping you'll write us now and then,
Jamie"—she nudged him—"to tell us what kind of a car you're
driving. About all the delicate young hearts you're breaking."
Jamie really wasn't that cute—his ears stuck out. But when I'd
remarked on that to Aunt Josie she told me not to be so per-
snickety. A smile that lit gray eyes to silver was a sign of rare
appreciation, a fine thing in a man.

Jamie got red and flustered, Aunt Josie teasing him in front
of everybody. But maybe it was partly because he didn't want

to leave Aunt Josie behind, didn't know how he'd ever have the nerve to meet any girls at all, or think of anything to say, without somebody to get him going. Then, as if she knew he was scared about leaving, right along with wanting to, she said, "Remember now. You can always come back if you get too lonely. We know you'll be pining."

They could scoff and howl at that, horse around. Declare that being there was something they could do without till the end of time, that they never wanted to see any old Farm again, always slaving, bossed around by old man Fiery. Worse than death itself. There was real fear in their eyes too, and I thought of the place under the corncrib where I'd heard some of them had been locked in—the worst parts they weren't saying. They did let off a lot of steam, though, raving about how terrible the Farm was, how they hated it and we knew they did, although everybody was grinning and Aunt Josie had told me that scarcely a one of them had a thing better to go home to.

When Ernie turned up the shelf radio he kept humming in the background, everybody stopped talking to listen. It was a special report: Three convicts had escaped from the penitentiary at Sand Isle. There was a guard dead, and they were armed and considered dangerous. Police were hunting all over the woods and setting up roadblocks. Killers on the loose. Now there wasn't any other sound in the place, all the boys transfixed. Cilly too, in the doorway, her red hands dripping against her apron. Taddy Barker had come inside for the first time, forgetful of Aunt Josie, his face as bloodless and fascinated as the rest.

Aunt Josie shook herself, calling across to Ernie, "Turn that thing down." Moving over to the jukebox to punch out some more music, she retrieved her Coke from the counter and motioned me to sit with her in a side booth, next to where some of the boys were. She shifted herself sideways, including them too.

"Think you'll be able to play Saturday, with that knee, Bill?" she asked, friendly, but he only shrugged. In the deep silence underneath Hank Williams singing "Cold, Cold Heart," I imagined that I too, along with those boys, was making a run for freedom, driving along the highway south of Sand Isle, driving with the river on one side, rock cliffs on the other, desperate in darkness. Once I got started running, I didn't know how to stop.

"Glory, that was a moony thing I picked out." Aunt Josie rolled her eyes. "See if you can do better." She gave me a nickel to do the honors, poking me out of the booth with her toe under the table. I studied the selections briefly and then chose "Five Foot Two," laughing when Aunt Josie did. Knowing she would, because it was an old joke between us. Once, when I wouldn't stop singing that song—getting it in my brain so I couldn't— she warned me what was going to happen. Then I did it on purpose too, and one day she let me have it with a pail of water when I came singing in the door.

"My, that tune does bring back memories," she marveled. "If I don't dance to it I'm likely to do anything," and she told Jamie he had to be her partner or she'd break his pitching arm. He hooted at that but let her coax him to stand up, shuffling his feet nervously, dodging nudges from the others. Still, he was on his feet, braver than the rest, which was partly why Aunt Josie thought he had so much on the ball. He took her instructions on where to lay his hands and started to move along with her in the cleared patch of floor before the flowing colors of the jukebox. They danced far apart, with Aunt Josie fooling most of the time, sighing and saying how romantic it was, winking at me. Though she was serious about teaching the fox-trot when "Careless" came on. Jamie's hand seemed scarcely to rest on Aunt Josie's waist, which wasn't visible under the loose cotton shift, and her hand on his shoulder was formal and graceful, while his face grew steadily more absorbed, rapt, knowing he was holding a woman in his arms.

After Jamie, Aunt Josie made all the boys take a turn, at least for a minute. She kept me hopping to choose music, and each boy got up, although they had to be prodded and teased forward, acting like they didn't want to. Aunt Josie didn't take any of it personally, as if she knew something that was truer. "How else will any of you know what to do when some pretty gal, like my niece here, wants to dance but needs somebody to show her how, give her confidence. Someday you'll look back and be glad. You'll remember." Already they looked almost glad, an arm's length from Aunt Josie, moving over the dark wooden floor while music was playing, almost dancing.

At last Aunt Josie was tired out and went back to the counter, declaring she ought to get the girls home to bed. Mary Jane was already asleep against the wall of a booth, while Nancy, the stuffed dog to herself, sucked groggily on its remaining ear. Ernie was watching Aunt Josie's legs swing beside the stool where she perched, white legs crossed to make me think of a forked birch branch. She never got any tan on them, she was that careful, and she praised them with a tireless pure satisfaction. They were unaccountably ornamental, considering the rest of her—she said that with a smile that belied the appraisal. When she caught Ernie admiring them she nodded, as though she knew exactly how he felt.

While she drank the rest of her vanilla Coke, Ernie leaned closer. "I'd lock up real good tonight, Josie. Some them boys been climbing out nights. Hellin' different places. This kind of thing, the break. I don't know." He shook his head, eyes shifting around the room. "You don't want no trouble, do you, Josie?" His eyes made it seem like it was the two of them against everybody else.

Aunt Josie got a smart look on her face, a boldness that rose up in her sometimes, like the hula girl sashayed across Ernie's arm. "I reckon I can handle anything that comes my way." Her eyes stayed narrow while Ernie turned a geranium red. Then she recovered her nice way. "Don't worry about us none. We're out for bear, aren't we, girls?" She scooped me up as she spun off her stool and together we gathered up the girls, who, cranky and stumbling, had to be carried to the door before they could be persuaded to walk by themselves.

"Some folks think this here's a Sunday school," Ernie said, but Aunt Josie didn't look back. "Sure enough," she said, calling good night behind her, the three of us now following along after her through the summer's mild night, fireflies starring the grass. Aunt Josie, sniffing like a hound, asked did we mind the smell of new-mown hay and wasn't the honeysuckle sweet. Telling us that the night before she'd heard a screech owl in the woods to the north. She used to hear them all night long on Coby Ridge. Following Aunt Josie on the tar walks that sucked at my bare feet, moving in and out of the lamplight and the moonlight, hearing her talk about old times, I was cultivating a fine lonesomeness, thinking about romantic things.

But the old tumbledown house loomed forsaken. At this hour it showed that no amount of enthusiastic devoted attention could ever mend it, and when we climbed the four wooden stairs to the porch our steps echoed, voices trailed out thin as thread. It could have been a hideout, deserted and secretive, although all around the Farm, unseen behind the trees, was the iron fence that made it a prison. Hurriedly, I got inside and, upstairs, wiped the girls' faces, hands, and knees at the bathroom sink, dropping their gowns over the line they made with their arms upstretched. Leading them, cross and complaining about tiny sores and bug bites, to their bed in the room at the back of the hall, I felt so tired then I let Aunt Josie tuck me in beside them, still in my shorts and blouse. Even then I felt alone, as though everything would be strange forever. More awake than sleeping, it seemed I was dreaming, driven through an urgent passage, not going toward anything but propelled fast away.

Sometime in the midst of my dreams a touch woke me. I sat bolt upright and Mary Jane said, "I'm scared," pulling at me. Nancy was crying softly, saying, "Mamma." They started down the hall after Aunt Josie, and I went with them. When they wanted their mother, no one else would do.

Aunt Josie was awake and sitting up when we came in the door. "Hush," she said to the girls, hugging them in her arms. I stopped everything, including breathing, listening through the cavernous house, hearing everything and nothing. "We'll go down," she said. "It's only the shutter banging. Come, girls." The leaves fluttering at the screen whipped my heart and I thought I wouldn't be able to go with her, but already I was stepping along the splintery floor, going toward the stairs. Going with Aunt Josie, just like she said.

"We'll all stay together," Aunt Josie said, and lit a match, appearing in the wavery, fluttering light in her usual sleeping garb, her shadow stabbing off the ceiling and running on the walls. Whenever shivering light streams over walls I see Aunt Josie naked by matchlight, but that night, hardly conscious, I descended along with her, now a candle held before us. Down the tunnel of the back stairwell we went, only her awesome composure making it possible.

In the airless kitchen, the stifling heat from the day, the musk of stale milk and damp-rot from the pantry sideboard, seemed as old as the house. Aunt Josie whispered, "We'll go all over. Stay with me." Nothing else would have been possible. She reached up and brought down the iron butcher knife Uncle Tim used for dressing chickens. He kept it sharp, stropping it along with his razor, laying it safe on the shelf above the wood-fired range. We gazed hopelessly at its massive blade, opaque as a stone.

The dining room loomed as enormous as the setting for a medieval banquet, the huge table that sat twelve, twelve oak chairs, along the wall the carved buffet. No breeze in there either, moonlight static in the air, the oily scent of tallow. From beyond the walls it seemed that ghosts held long, anguished sighs.

We filed on into the central hall, which rose with the staircase two floors overhead, everything bright from a high window as we arrived at the parlor door. What could be waiting there? Did someone think moonlight would just then begin to dance in the hall? Aunt Josie stood in the door holding the candle, and from behind her we saw her reflection in the parlor mirror. Magnificent, her breasts full pendant globes resting over her high-domed belly, around her the faded gowns of the girls billowing white in the draft-blown candlelight. Across the wall the shadow of the knife glanced darkly. My own reflection beside her was tall and staunch as a lance.

We didn't see who gasped, "Oh, Jesus," then scrabbled and slid over the sill, feet running on down the hill. "Who was it, who was it?" we asked, sticking close as Aunt Josie slammed the window shut and lit the gas jet—my Aunt Josie as I knew her, hair poking out the way scared hair does. Only she didn't seem scared now, more startled with the light coming on, seeing herself without clothes, and she took off for the bathroom.

"Some fool boys, I reckon," she answered our questions as we crowded behind her. "Trying to give us a turn. Well, all's well that ends well, though I suppose we'll get us a phone line. Maybe a dog. You'd like that, sweet blessed things," and she knelt and kissed the girls, tugging me to go along to check the house, secure the locks, and put the girls to bed.

Safe at last in the quiet and in-drawing house, Aunt Josie and I sat at the kitchen table, which was propped level with two books to overcome the sagging floor of the house that needed everything, Aunt Josie slicing cake. She licked the knife and declared she was perishing for want of nourishment, darting her eyes at me. Both of us knew she was breaking her diet and would be mad at herself in the morning.

"It could have been Ernie," I ventured as I stuffed my mouth with cake and milk, wanting her to know I was growing up, learning some of the things a woman needs to know.

Aunt Josie laid down the knife, looking at me closely while

she reached over to flick a piece of my hair. Admiring it always, although sometimes she allowed her own pleased her well enough since it was the only thing about her that was thin. "There's been more than enough excitement around here for one night," she declared. "In the morning we'll see what we can find out. But anyway," and she stretched her arms high in the worn-through pink gown she'd snatched from somewhere, no more shape to it than the dresses she wore, "I figure whoever it was, there's nothing so heart- and soul-satisfying to a man as a dream come true." And then she laughed, laughter soft and concealing as the whole mysterious night, and I felt glad and relieved and thought again of the five hundred boys mowing the grass, sleeping now up on the hill.

Crowing

SALLY STARES OFF at the barn, which is about a hundred yards beyond the two of them. At this distance and in the smolder of Indian summer, it appears to emanate an influence, seems about to wake and stir. Bleached out, silvered by the weather of all descriptions that sweeps these Northern mountains, built into and over the hillside, its slate roof gleams, dividing the light into converging patterns of green and red hexagonals.

Shout into his hearing aid, rouse up the old goat, Sally urges herself, the old man shuffling along at her side, at his chosen pace, chosen intentionally, she can't help feeling. Weariness begins to engulf her and she imagines lying down at the side of the road for a senile doze.

When Louisa asked her, Sally could have said no. "I don't want to impose," Louisa had insisted. "Only if you're not busy." Louisa's father was living with her again, after a brief convalescence in a nursing home. She needed someone to stay with him for just a couple of hours, and Sally assured her it would be fine. "My job doesn't start for another week. The kids will be in school. It'll be fun." That was stretching it; Mr. Austin's antics at the nursing home were unnerving to hear about, but then he'd wanted out of there. Now, by all accounts, he was happy and would presumably behave himself.

As though she'd read Sally's thought, Louisa added firmly, almost defensively, "I'm sure Dad won't give you any trouble. He hasn't had a drink since he came back." Let him take the long walk to the barn, where he could feed the animals, something he did every afternoon. Then he'd probably want a nap.

When Louisa introduced Sally, Mr. Austin took her hand in his and held to it firmly with a surprisingly forceful grip, his eyes foxy, holding her gaze. Gradually, when he didn't release her, she realized he was pressing her persistently backward, tilting her off balance. As she pulled upright he let go of her hand and pinched her cheek, declaring it was a good omen that her name was Austin too, the same as his. Sally kept her denials to herself, and her embarrassment; the name Austin was her husband's and Anglo-Saxon only because his father, in clothing still redolent of the herring of Riga, had chosen it from an encyclopedia.

Since Louisa left, their companionship has lagged, unpunctuated by pranks or flirtation. Walking the road with her now, the old man seems to sneak little breaths, quick moans of emphysema like echoes of the wild dove calls Sally hears all around them, and more distantly from the rafter slats high on the barn. She feels a moment of pity for him and restrains her impatience with a smile.

"Austin, heh?" he ruminates, turning toward her, his voice wrecked and also his yellow stubby teeth. A lifetime of the pleasures of tobacco. He relishes claiming kin and returns her smile.

Her patience grinds in her teeth. They are wearing away from that, especially at night when she sleeps, and she thinks she tastes in her mouth a pulverized enamel of self-restraint. "We're cousins, I guess," she humors him.

"I can put up with anything but his drinking," Louisa had confided. "Any of that and he'll have to go back. Fires and crashes in the night won't do."

"Yep. His name's the most powerful thing a man's got," Mr. Austin affirms. "Never give it to the devil." He chuckles over a rapid glance behind, as though he might raise a demon readily. In the clear light, Sally notices that the gray stubble on his face outlines a faint pointed beard.

"You wouldn't believe it now, how he was, even twenty years ago," Louisa's husband told Sally once, relating like a marvel the old man's vanished strength and influence. "When I was courting Louisa, her father took us to *La Bohème*, ordered the meal for the three of us, everything they had, caviar, escargots. The wine cost fifty dollars. When Louisa got up and left the table, I felt something drop on my arm like a band of iron: her father's small, elegant hand. I looked up and met his eyes. 'If I thought you were sleeping with my daughter, I'd kill you,' he said. 'I know you would, I know you would,' I said, waiting with his hand on my arm."

The road they walk to the barn is a town road, but it seems to be part of the farm, mostly a rutted dirt track with open meadow and woodland stretching to the mountains on one side, falling on the valley side to the river and farther mountains beyond. There's very little traffic along here, mostly a few morning and evening cars going to the development that's been put in on the ridge. Immaculately groomed, the farm is fallow, save for the rounds of hay mowing, and there's a garden, pasture for the few remaining animals. The family has lost purpose here, complains of the taxes and considers a move north. Their wealth hasn't diminished appreciably, but their pride has, and a fresh start would be invigorating.

Near the barn the dust on the road pools thick, slips and sucks around their feet like a liquid or folds of silk, their prints moiling even as they lift out of it. Sally's feet are gritty. She feels she's traveled a long way. All this time they are regarded steadily by an old stallion, the one horse the family still keeps for itself, out of attachment. He is secluded in his steep and stony pasture at the edge of the orchard, wears a snarl of burdock, goldenrod, and asters at his forelock. His shrouded eyes flicker, narrow as seeds. In his vigilance his withers tremble, his mane streams. He could be in motion, secretly. He seems to lure Sally to mount him for a leap over the stone wall, a ramble through meadow and woodland. From such a tryst, no one would return.

At first, coming beside the orchard, Sally reminds herself to step clear of the fallen apples rotting on the road. But there are hundreds; unavoidable, they dissolve and mush under her feet, gather the dust into burdening clods sticky with cider. Sometimes on fall days she is invited up to help turn cider in the antique hand press and, drinking cup after cup, feels tipsy for no other reason than the fresh, tingling bite of the green drink, its associations with distillation and must. Above them now, the apples still clinging to the trees dangle a carnival red against the sapphire sky, and she wishes she could amaze them, the horse and man, imagines juggling and dancing, the sun warm after the brisk September morning, the stallion's wreath cocked on his brow.

They arrive at the barn, the horse neighing and prancing behind the line of electric wire that pens him in, and Sally moves ahead of Mr. Austin, feeling her arms swell up, strong and capable, as she pushes aside the wide double doors. But as the sunlight slams into the dark stronghold she draws back and lets him go ahead. The smell and immensity of the place suggest a cavern; glimpsing the dim hanging intricacies of the lofts and stalls, she remembers, by contrast, the filthy shed where her husband kept his rabbits, a last attempt to feed and care for something other than himself. At the end, he'd left his old dog with her to die.

Mr. Austin becomes livelier as he begins his errands as stablehand, collecting feed pans, crashing the lid on the grain box, kicking open stall doors. He's picked up a pipe and has poked it, unlit, in his jaw. Moving from stall to stall, Sally follows him, breathing intentionally through her mouth until she grows used to the accumulated odors, wondering if rats will come out while they're around. She hopes Mr. Austin won't fill his pipe and light up, or she will have to ask him to put it out, something he might resent.

"Sixty-five head of my own at one time," he says, handing out grain to the five horses they board on the farm.

"At the school?" Sally encourages him. He swings his head around sharply to look at her, as though she's annoyed him. For years he ran an exclusive private girls' school near Quebec City. Louisa had told her that she always spoke French to her mother, although she and her sisters were sent to the States to be educated.

"You any relation to the Austins that live down to Rutland?" he asks abruptly, tit for tat.

Sally decides to address the difficulty about her name and get it over with. "My name's not really Austin, at least not anymore. I'm divorced." Probably he'll look down on her. She'd never be one of his little mademoiselles, although by now he doesn't sound as though he ever *"parlez-vous'*d" in his life. The horses stomp uneasily, peer over the low stable doors, startled by her, the outburst emphatic now that she's told him.

Mr. Austin seems to take the retraction of her name to heart, appearing more bent and rumpled in his outmoded street wear. A tremor rocks his hand holding the pocked enamel pan, as if she's withdrawn stability along with the only connection that makes her presence there comprehensible. The truth is out. Sally can almost see it pass visibly along the seamed webs at the window, hear it ring in the whistle of a train following the river in the valley below. Abandoned, he stands forlorn before a bucket of water drawn for the pig. She feels relieved, though, and stronger, and picks up the pail to do him a favor, heading toward the pig in the far back of the barn. Around corners and through a dim corridor where Louisa took her once, she finds the pen which is formed by the limestone foundation.

There's no window and the pig is only a snorting heaviness until, brushing the air for the light string, Sally pulls it and sees him behind the gate, garbage and damp straw to his knees. The gate seems irrelevant in paradise and he does give her a foolish grin, indulging his morbid preference. Broccoli stumps root in his garden, carrots dangle green fronds, the pig is an absurd pink, sacrificial among his victuals. He accepts her company affably enough, welcomes the water as his due. Louisa has offered her a ham when the deed is done. People say farm animals know when the hog butcher is coming. Somehow. Even the day before, they will be restive, off their feed, as though word of the appointment has reached them.

Almost as though she'd expected it, she sees the flask lying in a corner, half hidden under a leaf of hay. Perhaps a rake would reach there, but she sees nothing like that and decides to let it go. She'll keep the old man in sight and later tell Louisa he's up to his tricks. His daughter can take care of it. Sally couldn't bear to go in with the pig. Her thin shoes would smear and swamp. At the thought of the pig's warm vegetable breath she winces.

In her absence Mr. Austin seems to have rallied from his disappointment and is busy feeding the chickens, which are penned into a small stall near the front doors; the slanted light luminous with the dark all around reminds Sally of manger scenes in paintings from the Northern Renaissance. "Here, chick, chick," he coaxes, sifting grain on the floor before him. Two hens speed up close to his narrow-toed street shoes, where he stands in the open gateway, and he slams them with a direct hit into their faces, grabbing another handful of grain. Three others come forward as those he's hit draw back. He fires another blast, then keeps on lashing out as five more race in, pecking and wincing, to scavenge whatever they can. Some drag their wings coyly, wantons after the fresh grain. Mr. Austin moves farther into the pen and fires at the remaining hens clustered around the rooster.

Stalking and agitated, he has been watching but seems hesitant, making only abortive approaches toward Mr. Austin.

He falls back a little and ruffs his feathers into a billowing shawl. There is no expression in his painted eye as he skids into the fray, across the small yard, darting at the legs of the old man, which are lost amid the loose folds of his gabardine trousers. With his raised foot, Mr. Austin aims a driving blow at the rooster. Rasps, "Aha, try that, will ya?" The rooster scatters a few feathers with a squawk, recovers, then flies in again. At the exact moment he's calculated, the old man whams him full force with the grain. The rooster rebounds, draws himself proud for a turn around the pen, marching in goose-step, preening his feathers, letting the light burnish in the deep maroon shades of his display. Again and again the bird snakes out with his horny beak, a young tireless fellow, and each time the old man kicks out, in rhythm like a chorus girl. Though, as he fights, his breath wheezes, his face purples.

"Mr. Austin." Sally nudges him, seeking his left ear with the hearing aid. "This is childish." With one arm she tries to maneuver the plank gate away from him so she can close it, her skin scraping on the straw-and-dung-crusted rim.

"Hey!" he barks, intent on the rooster, which parades again, his beak thrusting like a single yellowed fang over the heads of his insensible brood scurrying in and out of the battle. Abruptly, Mr. Austin seizes the door from under her hand, shoving her off balance as he raises his leg to drive at his advancing foe. "Get out of the way," he snaps.

Her arm is scratched from the door, and when she feels the tingle of grit against the side of her cheek, she whirls around, only to see the old man's back. Furious tears rise, although she'd scarcely felt the grain which now has trickled onto her shoulder.

While Mr. Austin continues to amuse himself with the chickens, Sally eases down the stable and goes around to the pigpen. This time she isn't afraid, climbs in, takes the flask, and is back over the gate before she even glances at the pig, who is occupied rooting out tidbits. The flask hidden in her pocket, she returns to the front as Mr. Austin hurls the empty can of grain at the far stone wall of the pen. Amid the clucking and clatter he brushes off his hands on his coat, licks his crumpled lips with the brown spike of his tongue. Over his spectacles he grins at Sally, as if he sees more clearly without them. The light in his eyes gathers to points, like spurs. Behind him the rooster paces, displays, and begins to crow.

"Off to feed piggy his pumpkin," Mr. Austin announces, his anticipation evident. Besides a drink, Sally supposes he has something in mind for the pig, his step light as he turns the corner.

Chaff spins in the drafts blown along the receding stanchions and diverging halls of the barn. When Mr. Austin has disappeared, Sally pulls the barn doors closed behind her and steps outside. She wedges a bar crosswise through the two handles, leaning against the door, which is now securely locked. Although there are easily other ways out of the barn, she relishes the thought that at least briefly he will kick and rattle the door, struggle and have to realize what she's done.

Before beginning the walk back to the house, she pauses at the mounting post to take in the view, a light breeze raising up the dark hair on her arm into a fur. She'll wait for Louisa to come home, and if Mr. Austin returns first, she'll ignore him. Maybe he will take the promised nap. Probably, in broad daylight, he won't burn down the house. The river valley, hazy and floating far below, suggests the vast inland sea which once covered the region. There's no sound from the barn except the racket the rooster makes with incessant aggrieved crowing.

Then, after a brief interval, a rival crow comes rilling out of the cavity of the barn, and she's certain the rooster knows instinctively: this crowing is no fowl but is a cracked and reedy imitation. Breaking off and then continuing, the mockery bears no more resemblance to an actual crow than a pointed dress shoe to a spur. Insult enough, though, it seems to goad the rooster into a frenzy of pealing shrieks and she can imagine how he stands, plumes, tail, and all erect, a colorful rag mop in a gale.

The leaves on the apple tree curl and tilt, mottled with the rust and blight of wild untended orchards. Passing clouds draw the sun's edges on the cusp into a horned moon. From the hayloft, Sally hears the swing and grate of the grappling fork which dangles on a thick rope from the center beam, a hanged man in effigy.

She walks back to the barn and, lifting the bar from the door, places the flask upright on the mounting post. It waits there like a prize or a temptation, although it is neither. When she starts back on the road, the piebald stallion comes to join her, on the other side of the electric wire, stagy and good company, keeping pace through the dissolving apples and dust.

The Harrier

I SAW JACE over on the village street yesterday. He said his old dog had run away, run off into the woods outside town, maybe to die, the way an Indian melted into the forest when his time had come. Jace said he might be leaving soon too. He's been saying that for years, in some ways like his stray dog, a ragtag wastrel. And yet there is a bittersweet in that rapscallion, something fantastical and something plaintive. He made me feel for one long winter that going into his bed, although it was a place under siege, dangerous and even frigid, in an unheated cabin of a single room, a seven-mile hike from town, into the woods and onto a cliff, would have been worth the last part of myself. I passed through the raging of that desire, but still I looked back, as someone who has lost something—flawed but unexampled.

After it was over I avoided even a glimpse of him, was gone from the village all day at my new job, and if I had to stop for milk at the creamery, I used my car, went out of my way not to pass him, to evade his gaze fastening on me from behind a store window, to be gone when he came rapidly onto the street. Because I couldn't go with him, but neither was I so indifferent I could forget him. There was my husband too, no having the two of them at once.

From the first I was wary of Jace. He had a quality about him, loose and free-rolling as he might appear, that I could imagine taking hold and never letting go. By turns he let his hair cascade to his shoulders, then shaved it to the bone. He could guzzle a keg of beer; then I'd seen him lurch into the variety store to purchase more. Other times he'd disappear into the woods with nothing. While underneath he was always just the same, a fire of grass and lilies.

I didn't go with him up into that bed in the forest, not in the end, although as I said, in that winter of cold and driving spikes of ice he seemed to slam against my bedroom window all night like some night bird wanting in. But I chose to lie on, hugging the curve of my husband's unyielding back, dreaming the smell that is feverish and rank, the distillation of roots and vines newly turned over. If I whispered, "Do you love me?" my husband answered from the other side, over the hump of his shoulder, "Compared to you, I don't give a damn for anything."

When in the night I couldn't sleep, I would get out of bed onto the cold floor, walk out to the colder kitchen, and stand, shivering, against the long window. The night would mass black, the frosted railings crystal lacework, and the stars marked points in time where, before I turned away, I could glimpse early extinctions. Back then to the bed, turned away, feeling stars collapse inside.

All winter I ran away from Jace, stayed beyond his reach, going for last-minute groceries to the IGA declining on the side street, losing its business day by day, rusty heads of lettuce, the moldy cucumbers rolling in the bins where I rooted for an onion or a potato. That was the store where Jace wouldn't come, though, and in those days it was risky for me even to see him. Even though I'd made up my mind. I knew his habits from watching him before. Knew the time of evening when he stopped for his beer, the scrap of food that would see him through another day. His diet was not so much strict as meager, as if he'd learned he could get further advantage out of life hungry. It was surprising how seldom I saw him, in such a small town. It showed how little we had in common, I thought, comforting myself.

Sometimes I misjudged and he would be there on the street, tall, with vapors of the ethereal trailing in his eyes, frail in the purple of early evening, that mist of winter twilight on snow where there are mountains. Still wearing the worn navy pea coat, flapping open, his body insubstantial and then unmoving when he saw me, his unguarded eyes fixed until I passed beyond him. Straight ahead I walked with Jace like that, willful as ever. But I wouldn't, and he had to let me go, my hands burning, streaming wildfire, keeping him away, while my frame held rigid as a post until I would be trembling, when I let myself, after I had left him. In the general store under the hanging bulb, drained into a pool on the dark oiled floor, I had to pause a moment to remember why I was there. I told myself those times, "Well, it's not over. Not yet."

Jace had come to our village about the same time as the commune. One summer day they were there, the girls gliding the walks in long calico skirts, barefoot, the boys racing down Main Street, trick-riding motorcycles, dancing on the corners, calling out to anybody, lifting beers, and grinning even at high noon. When one of them spoke to me I smiled back, because I couldn't help myself, and once a boy grabbed me and spun me around, releasing me with a slight bow. That was the first time I noticed Jace among the rest, although after that he was the one I always saw.

There was gossip from the first too, talk about the commune being run out of town. It wasn't decent, people said. Most of them lived together in the abandoned feed store by the railroad tracks, and men who went there, to make deliveries or sometimes on pretext, said the girls answered the door in various states of undress. Called "Come in," the same as if it were a cathouse. Propped on open windowsills, they were bold with anybody passing by. Town kids, and sometimes their fathers, would crawl down through the trash and weeds by the railroad bank to spy into the barn from the dark, the windows misted gold with kerosene light. Mornings at the post office I'd hear talk, merchants complaining about vagrants, veterans resentful of draft dodgers, although I never knew if there was any truth to that. Women I knew didn't let their young daughters walk over to town, didn't want them watched or discussed by those boys, who could stand on the street, forever it seemed, in perfect unyielding indolence.

But before the summer had ended, the commune had moved on, dissolved maybe. No one knew what became of them, as no one had known their origin, just there and gone, as if a plague of locusts had eaten their fill and blown away. A few sons and daughters had been lost to that visitation, which was what the townspeople had feared from the beginning. Although some of the older men realized another danger in the loose, narrow-hipped young men lounging in front of the village stores, so quiet and nonchalant, watching the wives go in and out. They knew there is nothing ever really quiet in a young man.

The commune left something too. It left Jace, and a few stragglers, a few woebegone girls. Jace stayed on at the edge of the railroad tracks, on a rutted back road, and kept up the on-and-off-again mechanic shop that kept him on-and-off-again busy. He could, when he had a mind to, fix about anything, and gradually farmers and tradesmen from around town began going to him with cars and machinery, defensive at first, making it clear when they praised Jace that he was a different breed from the others, wasn't afraid of work. Though they still wouldn't want him eyeing their daughters, speaking to their wives. Jace never seemed to care, though. He already had more female company than he asked for, and I thought, when I knew him better, that all along he was looking for something else.

The first time Jace came into the church's secondhand shop, where I was volunteering my time, I didn't let on I'd ever noticed him before. After all, I was seven or eight years older, a married woman, no one to lose her head over a young man seen on the street laughing with pretty girls, passing joints openly back and forth. Sometimes he'd be sooty-black, from his blast furnace, I guess, and once he wore the whitest shirt I'd ever seen, cut with full sleeves and a gathered yoke, tucked into his jeans, with a silver belt. I could never forget how he looked, like no one else, flapping some variation of his mismatched clothing, which anywhere else would seem the last holdout from desolation, but on him looked like the right thing, something he might have studied for the effect. In summer he was barefoot, and then in the cold he might have a boot secured by a rag tied at the instep, a vest cut from a ratty fur coat.

That Wednesday afternoon in winter, Jace came into the shop, finding me at work. I did different things in the community, staying busy that way, and at home kept a large garden, canned and froze what I grew, baked bread, raised a few chickens in an old shed. I had taught school before, since the start of my marriage, but now I wanted to be at home and have a baby, hoping that my husband would look up from his desk, to which he clung so earnestly, to concede the emptiness I felt, that he might think he would like a baby too.

I was sorting through a pile of pilly polyester castoffs, most of them ugly rather than worn. In fact, that clothing has a kind of indestructible persistence as permanently trashy, best burned or transformed back into the petroleum from which it was concocted. There was a shadow, drastic and wintry, moving on the floor, and I looked up to see Jace in the doorway, lean, his limbs rangy, his hair a tunnel of wind-licked curls, eyes with the cloudy finish of watered silk. From the energy of him I feared for my life. His smile said, "I'll be anything you want, friend, pusher, lover": arrayed in his erratic patchwork, amused, eyes taking in everything. Next door saws buzzed from the furniture shop, and the splintering of opened wood rent the air.

"I hear there's a true spirit of charity here," he said.

"Sometimes," I said, and dropped my eyes to a table of children's overalls I began sorting and folding, finding the few not irretrievably stained or buttonless and strapless.

He came in and strolled about the tables, looking stuff over fast, already familiar with the selection. "Seen you around." I looked up when he said that. It was the first time I'd seen him fasten his attention and I thought, even that very first time, that he was asking, "Are you happy? Can I do anything for you?"— questions I wouldn't have known how to answer. But it's the kind of attention from a man that makes a woman, a woman like me, go quiet on the inside, and still, the water under deep ice. I aimed to cover my feelings, reaching out quickly to shake his hand and introduce myself.

"You're a fine-acting, fine-speaking woman." He laughed and on the spot picked out a rare find, an old cotton sweatshirt, pulling it over his head and paying me the fifty cents. After that he came in every Wednesday, considered the wares, and talked, asking me what I was up to, talking about people we both knew, the town government and zoning, the fight to keep the old roads closed, about the house he was building for himself up in the woods. He had taken apart the old Phillips barn, piece by piece, after the farm was sold for a car wash and gasland, carried away the beams, windows, and salvaged slate, all the materials he would need for his own place. Jace came in to visit me, I'd think, not for consolation or female sympathy, as another man might, but to see if he had missed something, and there was something confessional too. He would report how much he'd drunk the night before, how far he'd sailed through the air on the bike jump at the sandpit. The little bit of work he got done some days. He didn't seem proud or ashamed. It was more as if he was monitoring himself.

I never let myself expect anything from Jace, coming as he did from a world of careless pleasure and instant satisfaction, straight from the unmired bed, from the guiltless and swift consummation that was his right. He came into the dumpy little shop of castoffs and stained carpeting, crammed with its sad broken toys and ruined toasters, swinging with the feral grace of something in its natural state.

"Why should you work more than you do," I said once. "You have what you need."

He shrugged. "Sometimes I like to step out. I think about making things. Something simple, you know. A chandelier with a hundred candles."

"That's simple?"

"You got to have sparkle when you dance." He held out his arms as though I would fit into them for a waltz. I thought of the long-haired girls coming by, content with whatever he offered, and turned away.

"Today's the day I'm going to take hold," he announced. "Make some of the things I've never made before. Put this nose to the grindstone," and he gripped his nose in two fingers and yanked himself out the door. "I like being with you," he called, and from the window I watched him bounce along over the tracks on his heavy-duty Schwinn, fitted with rattraps he'd fashioned for the pedals. Right then I wanted him to have all the sparkle in the world, women, and a yard-lot of steel. His old dog lumbered up from the porch and padded after him.

Only after Jace had been gone for another week did I think about wanting him, about his wanting me. I pretended that he did, for I didn't know whether he ever wanted anything he didn't have. I never thought any further than that, his body and his desiring me—a little while, for I knew he came to a woman running like a freshet loosed in spring. Natural, turbulent, and random, changing course with the night's cold and the sun's slant.

A winter afternoon of thin sunlight sweeping on the floor, clouds coming in, Jace leaned in the door until I looked up. I smiled at him over the mound of blankets for the mission, looked away. I didn't know what might be in my eyes.

"You hear about the zoning meeting?" I asked, to hear myself saying something in the silence. "Will Beattie had some kind of seizure and had to be rushed to the hospital. There's no way he can put twenty houses in that meadow. It's all rock ledge."

"He's not village trustee for nothing."

"He says he'll put in a pipeline if he has to. Pump the sewage up to another field he owns farther up, into a holding tank."

"I'd like to make him a holding tank." Jace gritted his teeth and went white, as if he'd loosed some vision of destruction, and I regretted my vehemence, thinking of that man restrained, stuck full of needles and tubes.

"It's his land," I said, and went to the window overlooking the alley. A wet snow began, blurring the flashing blue-and-white of the birds eating seeds and suet across in a yard.

"It's all going down the drain." Jace spoke from close behind me, as if the birds were having their last meal, and the smaller birds did scatter when a large black one came and began to eat, the snow falling over its head in a hood.

"I'll make something for you," he said, his face near, sheer lavender hollows under his eyes. He looked spent, as if he didn't know anything more about living than I did. I wanted to ask why and what for. How long could he live on seed and other people's leavings?

A couple of days later I took my car down to his shop to be repaired, to ask him to weld the bumper onto the dented and rusted frame of the ten-year-old Citroën which had come to me cheap. Somebody else's wreck. I drove the short distance down, turning left after the tracks and continuing on the snow-covered dirt that degenerated further into frozen ruts, barely missing a hovel which hatched children in batches who came to school smelling to high heaven, all of them in need of remedial classes. I'd tutored some myself, volunteering my time. The track ended in front of the old station house, abandoned now by the railroad, freights whizzing right through town with a whistle blow, like a flick of saucy tail. A short distance beyond was a warehouse I presumed was Jace's shop, and I parked where the snowplow had stopped, and walked over.

It seemed no one was around and I moved the polished lock on the front just barely, expecting to leave, and glad of it, when a voice shouted, "Go round." A path led to the side and the dog was at the door, brindled and shaggy. I supposed he'd had no shots. But he moved his tail in a friendly thumping and I went inside, into the high-raftered room, which was open and clean-swept, all around brick walls rising, with wide banks of factory windows, at the top the pitched roof gabled in wood. Jace was under an old tractor, his legs coming out in their jeans on the oil-spotted cement. Right then I wanted to lie between them.

"Howdy," he called over the sputter of whatever he was doing, sparks showering around him. "Be right there." He had no idea who I was, friend or foe.

Don't hurry, don't hurry. I turned from his legs and paced the circumference of the room, examining his few hung tools, the remains of a rusted muffler in the corner, ninety-nine beer bottles lined neatly along the walls. Marijuana grew under an ultraviolet light. As I'd imagined, Jace traveled through the world as footloose as the wayfaring dog, except for those few props, which could as easily be exchanged for others. Then it was quiet, Jace scooting out from under the tractor. I turned to watch his hips and the rest of him emerge. His arms shoved him upright. I realized he'd been clean-shaven before, recognized now in a shadow of new beard webbed on his cheeks. His clothes—I could not imagine washing them or doing anything for him. All that long body, and his blue eyes rippling in snow light, drenching me.

"Risky business. Welding gas tanks. Old-timers did them full up with gas. That was the trick. What brings you here?" He stood with the cooled torch, waiting, the poise of a seasoned loiterer.

"My car. It needs a tune-up and the bumper's falling off. Somebody jumped on it, I guess. Not to mention the rust."

"Lady, I'm your man." He turned and went before me to the door. It was as though I followed him with a bundle banded to my forehead over a forest path, my feet in deerskin. My car pleased him, the old wreck that had been declared totaled in an accident before I bought it for forty dollars, and he walked around it with folded arms. "Let me at it," he decided, and threw his arms out, his head back, and it was as though he meant that for me.

"When can you do it?" I asked, sticking to business. He leaned to consider, drinking from a beer he'd carried outside. "Now's okay." So just like that he went to work, on the spur of the moment, nothing else to do.

I walked home, wondering if I would have to come back and dig the car out of the mound of junk edging into the woods behind his shed, but the next noon Jace appeared at my door, whirling keys on his finger, his mouth red, like a flame painted on a car, amid his darkening beard. When he glanced into the swept and ordered kitchen, he bent over and removed his boots, set them by the door. It was the time of the winter thaw which always came, sooner or later, the melting water puddling onto the snow cover, compressing it, until sagging and decayed it would freeze again in the returning cold. Around the trees in the yard the air swirled with mist and it seemed, from the corner of my eye, I could see the southern wind.

"I see you keep house like a goddamn white woman." He nodded. "I never smelled bread that fresh or saw tomatoes so pretty." I had brought some from the cellar and they glowed on the counter like tulip heads under water beside a jar of green pickles.

"When I left home I left everything," he said, and aged in that second, closing the gap between us, showing what leaving had cost. "Some would say they threw me out. Praise be." He shook his hands in the air for mockery, driving expulsions down into the dark. "Bring out your tea, lady. I'm ready to celebrate. Home again."

"I only have tea bags." I apologized for Lipton's. The commune had sold a homegrown mint tea.

"That's cool." He was quiet, sitting at the window before the slide and pause of watery snow, colored pearl and silver on the glass; the rain and drizzle, just another circumstance like everything, all right with him. I felt I could never do enough for him, or too little.

"Show me where your place is." I stood by the table, waiting while the water heated. It felt safer to stand, as if I might have to run out of the house to escape.

"Over there, across. Beyond Miller's Hill. Past the gravel pit and on. Another few miles up that next rise. I've had my eye on it since I first came up here."

"Do you want something to eat?" I asked, pouring the boiling water. I thought he might eat, tentatively, something ritually purified or raw.

"Anything's fine. When I was with the macros it was rice, green things. Whatever's handy."

"How'd you get with them—if you weren't with them, I mean?"

"I came to see the country. Heard about it from my mother, all the way from hell in New Jersey. Her people were from here." He ate a slice of bread, slowly, his hands clean except for the stains around the fingernails, imbedded grease. He told about coming up to New England, riding with a friend here and there, staying with people somebody knew. Sleeping in fields. They found shelters on the Appalachian Trail. "One day, near Lincoln Gap, just cruising along, high on something, I came across Pepe's place."

"Pepe Rainbow, the sculptor?"

"Out in the middle of this field was a shitload of steel, big as a landslide. 'Stop the car.' It spoke to me. I jumped out, whooping and hollering. A guy on the porch, up the road, feet on the railing, was staring. I yelled, did he know the meaning of that monstrosity. He says he'd be the last to know, since he put it there. I told him it looked like the beginning and the end, the place of waterless desolation. He like to split a gut."

Jace was eating, polite, with his napkin on his lap, and I was thinking of him in my bed, in a field of wildflowers, hanging out both ends. Too big, his cheekbones channels of stone, buckled by immense pressure. It seemed an immense distance down inside a man, utterly convulsive, for a man is more than his flesh and bone, the fine blue throb at the vein.

"I heard things," I said, "about the commune."

"You believe everything you hear?" He was serious, leaning over the table, as if with his will he could form me into something not seen since the beginning of time, his hands gripping the table, those hands that could take iron and bend it into flowers. "I want to take you to my place."

I heard the rain, freezing now, striking against the glass. He would take anyone with him. Girls had been there on his mattress at the shop, the bed at the top of the ladder, waiting like his body. Strange that a man should dress in tatters and make his bed so neat.

"Pepe taught me everything. We worked all day, sweated out the nights. Did a million cars, inside and out. That old furnace was a red-hot number. We had ourselves an exhibit. Up at his place. Lasted forty days and forty nights." He eyed me as if he felt me stir and could gentle me with a word. "A regular art gallery.

"We'd go to the junkyard. Jump a stack of rolled cars and start to rip. Take it in sheets. Pepe taught me that—to work steady and take it whole. The fuck with measuring and creeping. Burn right through." I felt that way under the moving of his eyes. He would have to take me with my beating heart, my body going ragged at the core. I drank tea, the cup rattling in the saucer.

That night I looked toward the place he'd shown me, across the river and into the mountains, where he lived in the woods. Maybe he was there now, where I could have seen, if I could see through rocks and earth. I imagined his house, an airy frame of filigree swinging from the trees. Coy dogs ran those woods in packs, brought down the winter-starved deer and ate them while they struggled to run on, pumping their hearts onto the snow. In the last century a man had found the tusk of a mastodon. Even now there might be an improbable beast, moving on unseen. I watched and watched to see some beacon in the forest, some indication of a human presence, but there was only the cold surging back, dropping over the land.

In bed again, I whispered to my husband, "Don't you think we could have a baby?"

Disturbed from his sleep, his voice came over his shoulder: "Don't you ever quit?" Then he was sorry, saying from the dark, "We can't for a while. You've got too much time on your hands. Maybe you should go back to work for a while." Waiting in the dark, just out of reach, were all the babies I would never have, the lovers I would never hold. He turned around me then under the heap of winter blankets and put his arm along my hips. I felt below the involuntary little rise, and then we lay still while outside I heard the gale of wind tearing at the house, its sob, while no light shone.

In the morning I told my husband about Jace and his work, how he fixed cars and made art out of junkyard heaps. "Why don't you have him make that chandelier you've been talking about?" he said.

"I'll see. Maybe, if I run into him." It was better not to, but my husband took matters into his own hands, throwing us at each other. "I'll ask if you don't. I want you to have it."

I dressed in first one outfit, a skirt and blouse, then changed to jeans, then back to a skirt. It was as if desires revolved before me on a pedestal, begging, "Choose me, choose me." The rain had frozen on every surface, icing trees and roofs, wires, last summer's grasses, the world revealing its heart at last. Overdressed, overwrought, overcold, I arrived at Jace's shop, knocking and turning the door handle at once, tromping in. The burnt-out furnace stood cold as a sentinel at dawn. The old dog assembled itself for a welcome as I looked up to the top of the ladder, greeting contempt full face. Jace's sleepy face twitched above the railing, contending with the conflicts inside him. Over his naked shoulder another face hung, disembodied. Pale hair swept all around.

Although I had no right, I felt my face twist like something thrown away. He was coming down fast, after me, violent in his thickening beard and haste. Let him fall, I thought, heading for the outside and standing there, exposed like the two or three iced leaves on a bramble bush, leaves that would not accept their fate.

"Surprise," Jace said, a bitter wind in his teeth. He stood in front of me, shading his eyes, for the sun scattered shrapnel of light off the ice forest. Our having met before seemed as un-natural as my being there, standing in the stalk-stiff weeds and ruts, trash at my ankles, as my ever counting on anything from a wolf-boy.

"Laura," he was saying, and I waited, light bursting in the trees as the melt began. "I could blow all this." He shrugged to include everything. I nodded my head, one way or another, want-ing to get away.

My car lurched and sprang past the tied dogs that guarded the cold sniveling children adrift on the road. I knew some of them slept on a dirt cellar-hole floor, got up in the dark to do chores at a nearby farm. I didn't feel safe again until I was back on the main thoroughfare, where goods had been bought and sold for a hundred and fifty years, and before that—traded, carried along the rivers and through the forests on immemorial paths. It was a settlement, where people wanted things and clung to them desperately.

But Jace was at my door soon after I got home, the dog at his heels, ice melting and dripping into wavelets, icicles shattering on the porch floor. Streams gushed from the roof onto his face and hair—his eyes like a wild appeal dashed off in ink, not yet dry. "Come with me," he said. And of course I was going, for how else could I reply to something flying overhead and crying out, to the pacing of beasts beyond the fire, my own scent drawing them.

We left town by the iron bridge that had been inadvertently laid in backward by feckless engineers after the flood of '32, splashed through salt pools from the runoff, stagnant atop frozen snow, salt that would by spring soak down into roots and wells, the earth saturated to the salinity of human blood, so that finally it might rise and scream. Then the dirt road, sloppy and rutted, the railroad track running beside us and away. I had let Jace drive my car, as if to convince myself I had been abducted by force, carried captive across a wasteland. "I've made you something," he said. In the back the dog lapped at the rushing air.

We passed the most recent, farthest outreach of modern development, seventeen raised ranches lined along the road, their blank stares aimed at the village and the western mountains. The hasty exit of the developer had left Mountain Vista another dependent on the town, the water giving out and the old town road unsuited to school bus travel. Not a tree left standing.

It was gone then, the land spreading free and open, and I felt the rising intensity which holds the nerves still and comes from the apprehension of distance flowing into distance, on and on.

It was serenely clear, no taint of civilization or development, only the roll and pitch of the earth going on into the untroubled and unruined land that was peaceful under the sky and mountains.

They loomed beyond the rain and thaw and drip which mucked the low roads, pocking the snow in its dip across the meadows into the thickets of hemlock and spruce. It was as if I had been waiting for mountains, as the hope flutters still that there is some escape, something that means more than just working and sleeping, getting and spending. Jace has his home here, I was thinking, and it was while I was thinking this, no interval in between, that I realized where I was. Between us and the mountains and the extending plateau, a chain-link fence rose fifteen feet high, twined and interlaced with brambles and dead vines, the top lashed with thick barbed wire. A fence—we were turning off and parking then—a fence that established a barrier to anything that would invade that preserve, as though something shameful were hidden there, the land kept safe because its purpose was not preservation but annihilation. The government warned everybody away in red letters, warned trespassers they would be blown to kingdom come.

I sat in the car, staring at the fence as though it penned me in. On test days I could hear the explosions from the village. Gunfire from the testing range, guns destined for Vietnam. "Why here?" I asked Jace, embarrassed, as if I should know.

He shrugged and paused as if the question were difficult, his eyes averted. "It's free." Getting out of the car he slipped on the slick snow and caught himself flat on the hood with both arms. While I still sat there, watching him through the windshield, he carefully pushed himself upward, teetered mid-arabesque, then turned to start up the hill on a path worn among the trees, winding under rock outcroppings, going on up to somewhere on the hillside across from the U.S. Army Testing Range. The dog had already made a beeline for home, raising some hell. I heard him bay. That was the only sound in that vast stillness. Some days it must have been deafening. Up on the ledge where Jace was headed, a very large bird could hover, heaving burdensome wings, watching with a farsighted gaze that could reckon a mouse at a hundred feet, amid myriad acres of mountain and snowfield.

Jace was all that moved. I watched him climb, not looking back, the worn shine of his navy pea coat lapping in wingbeats around his faded jeans, his legs thin and rapacious, gathering speed, lifting in a cadence of upward momentum toward his perch on the cliff. I wondered what he had made me. All I could imagine was an ingot of iron.

Then he was gone, as though I'd dreamed him up in a mist of yearning and knew him now as he was meant to be, alone before a circle of stones, hunched over a meager blaze just sufficient to warn other scavengers drawn by the light. A drifter who gave only the appearance of drifting, he had come with unerring aim, a harrier drawn to prey upon the end of things.

The Whole of the World

THEY ALWAYS TOLD IT that Daddy came home just as night was falling down through the oak trees and bats were swooping low to feed. Mamma had stayed upstairs for a while with a camphor rag tied around her forehead, but then she decided to rise to the occasion and returned to the kitchen to look once more at the fried chicken which was dry as meal in the warming oven.

That was when the women first heard the footsteps running on the gravel, and the two grown daughters went out onto the porch. They were hoping and praying it would be at least one of the men, and they were standing right there watching when Daddy came around the corner of the house. He had his arms pumping as if he were making his way through water, they said later, and his face looked red and tough, so they figured he must have been running a long time even though his breath was calm and didn't sound out loud. But with his red face and the fiery crisscross latticing his naked chest and his legs below the blue swimming trunks, and even his freckles showing all over, it had to have been earlier than they told it, or how could they have seen everything in living color. Still, they swore they could, while at the same time they remembered his pale hair glistening silvery in the porch light with the dark all around.

No one had heard the police car pull up out front. There was just the dog barking in the distance and the sound of running footsteps after Daddy got out of the car. They made extra noise because of the heavy army-issue combat boots Daddy wore. He didn't have on any socks. They knew that for certain.

"Daddy!" The two daughters were shrill in relief. "Daddy!" Mamma stayed in the kitchen, pretending something, maybe indifference, but there was so much feeling coming from her she might as well have been right out in the thick of things, going with her daughters down the long stairway into the yard.

"Well, if it's not my own two daughters," Daddy answered back, pumping on around the yard a second time with his head thrown back, fading into dusk, his face tearing off quick wild looks, every now and then giving a spring. It looked as though once he was running free he might not be able to stop at all and would go on and vault the picnic table and dip into Mrs. Bowers's birdbath.

Sally Drew spoke first, for her sister who stood speechless beside her. "Marie's worried sick about Becky."

"She's with Tom," Daddy answered, as if that was all right. "Now, go and tell that old woman to hang dinner and get out here. Give a proper welcome. The lost is found, the prodigal returned." He sprinted around the corner of the house. Now they didn't even hear the dog.

That was when Marie recovered the strength of her legs and walked farther into the yard, her step like Mamma's when she had left the kitchen for the bedroom. Her face was braced in the hell-bent way it used to be when Daddy wouldn't quit asking her boyfriends how much money they earned, and sometimes he made them Indian-wrestle. When Daddy came back in sight, over by Downey's house, he took one look at Marie and started hopping backward in mock fear. Then when he stopped short she nearly landed on top of him.

"Daddy, I'm asking you once and then I'm calling the police. Where is my daughter?" Marie's voice was desperate and Daddy replied in sober contrast, "I tell you, girl. She's with Tom. Anyway, the police have already been here. Remember, they brought me home."

"Then where is Tom? Are they all right?"

"Last I saw was three, four hours ago. At the quarry. They were fine then. That I can vouch for."

"Three, four hours. And now it's late. I can't believe I ever trusted you." Marie's voice rose and fell while frantically she kneaded the life out of her folded arms, walking a circle around the picnic table.

Sally Drew went down the steps and stood before Daddy. "Have you been in a fight? And where are the rest of your clothes?" She had her hands on her hips.

Daddy shook his head. "I thought one of you might inquire about your husbands. But no, it's children and property first." He turned away and walked off, not with the high stride now, but caved over in a slouch, going to the picnic table, where he sat down with his back to the dishes and tableware and to his white-painted brick house, which, he maintained, only a fool would have bought.

It was then that Colin's car came, full tilt along the drive, the gravel hissing. Even before he was stopped, Tom jumped out of the car and yelled, or started to, "Have you seen?" while Colin stayed at the wheel, just watching. Then Tom saw that his wife's daddy was sitting there, big as life, facing out toward the hedge between them and Bowers's striped awnings, on the edge of the bench, with his legs spread open, his back to them. Becky came skedaddling from the car, into her mother's arms, where she burst out crying as she buried her face. Up until then she'd been half smiling, as though she was having fun or thought she ought to be.

Tom glanced over toward Colin, or toward where he'd been, sitting in the car, though now Colin was grabbing Daddy by the arm, saying, "What the hell! What the hell!" soaring tall over Daddy in the cowboy boots he wore when he wasn't in his bedroom slippers. Daddy was smoking steadily, had been doing so almost since he was eleven, no matter what else was happening or what they were doing to him. Paying no attention to Colin's grip, he stood up, and Colin let him go, Daddy's face getting more and more the look he got playing cards, knowing he was going to outsmart the rest of them, one hand tied behind. He dealt his silver-coin smile.

"Just what are you going to do about it? I always said you were some precious variety of pantywaist mamma's boy." Then Daddy sat again, as though the lack of any real competition in the world or hope for it had done him in. Abruptly—maybe something had snapped and she'd lost interest—Marie turned her back and carried Becky into the house.

"Pantywaist." Colin's voice wailed as if he was indeed just that, and it seemed as though everyone for miles would hear. That brought Mamma out on the porch for the first time, though she still didn't look directly at Daddy, refusing to show any surprise, come what may. Sally Drew went over to stand beside Colin, but his business was still with Daddy, and he moved off to face him, the picnic table between them, with Colin's hands set like he might tip it over.

Daddy simply got up and walked across the yard to drink from the hose, leaving Colin alone at the table, where he leaned his head in his hands. The flood from the porch lighted up the table with the dark all around and left the impression that it had been fully dark when Daddy first came home. They were only certain of darkness after that, except for the shine of the flood and the kitchen light from the Bowerses'.

Mamma resigned herself, speaking from the high porch like Juliet. "We may as well eat," and went inside, while Daddy decided to take a shower and held the hose on top of his head. The women carried the food outside, bringing the chicken in the pan from the oven, the parsley potatoes gone gray and soggy, the overboiled fodder beans with salt pork. They had to walk on eggs to avoid tripping because of the experimental grass plugs Daddy had set in. He was trying to raise some real grass back in there where the oaks hung so thick mold was growing on the ground itself. It was perhaps a vain hope to cover that confined suburban lawn with a perennial grass native to East Asia, but it spoke to Daddy. The wasted effort and heartbreaking failure reminded him of the dream he'd once had, of farming the rocky hillsides of his West Virginia home. He expected setbacks and tended his exotic crop with a solicitude he'd never betray to humans.

Mamma came to the table last of all, carrying the tray of iced tea, almost black, her specialty, along with the yellow cake she generally served for dessert, and they began to eat. The chirr of the frogs from the wet place down by the abandoned streetcar tracks made a din that was enthralling, while in their silence the moths banged at the floodlight, killing themselves.

The impress of Mamma's sharp little teeth working on her chicken wing manifested a restraint they all felt, uneasiness afflicting the whole table. Finally, when she couldn't help herself, she said, "You might have worn your shirt to the table, Henry."

"I don't have it," Daddy answered. He went on eating, fast and a lot, having a second helping before Mamma was half finished with her first. There was plenty of food, Tom the only other one with any appetite, and when he was hungry he didn't seem to notice what he was eating, just getting it down. When Daddy swallowed off his tea and then peremptorily drained Mamma's in one gulp without asking, everyone looked up, Mamma fixing to speak her indignation when she was through looking it. But Daddy said, "That was the only time in my life I was ever lost in the woods." A rift opened in his voice that made it seem Daddy might cry out loud, something he'd never done before either, not that anyone knew.

Tom said, "Some of us could say the same." He didn't sound angry but wry and curious, as if, home and fed now, he was beginning to wonder what had happened to Daddy that day, what had become of his clothes. Which just went to prove what Daddy said, that if Tom couldn't be reading and underlining some textbook, he couldn't care less what he was doing. Would probably just as soon be lost in the woods.

"That was the point," Daddy said. "You were meant to be lost. I wasn't." He met everyone's eyes, not giving an inch.

"No good coyote," Colin said, and stood, getting all worked up again, with his fingers showing pale, gripping the redwood table.

"I can call names too, sonny," Daddy met him. Asking Colin—just how far do you want to take this? He didn't have to threaten him outright, because they all knew from experience how far Daddy would go. Colin removed his glasses, wiping them on his shirttail, a face pallid as barley corn. Then he put them on again.

"He wasn't ever any different," Mamma said to anyone who would listen.

"Why, old woman. Found your tongue, have you?" Mamma thought better of it and dropped her eyes.

"Let's just try to have a nice time," Marie said. "Everything's turned out all right." She'd come back from feeding Becky and putting her to bed, looked about done in herself.

"You were always the sweet one, daughter," Daddy said, not giving a hoot for sweetness. Again they heard the frogs from the bottomland by the tracks, in a steady, reedy drone behind the sharp talk, part of the net that kept them there under oaks and stars. Up there, beyond the world, starlight trailed, celestial figures held in an inverted sea.

"Henry." Mamma spoke up again. "Haven't you done enough? Ruined my dinner, worried everybody to death?"

"Typical. A time like this and all you can think about is your confounded dinner. Sometimes you amaze me. Mystery, adventure—the tenor and tenacity of your mind remind me of nothing

so much as my unremitting battle against crabgrass." Mamma
looked around as though for help, then gave a jittery little smile,
capitulating to his boundless superiority and the sad truth that
no one would help her.

"That's the proper spirit. A loving wife glad her husband is
home." Daddy glared around to see everyone being glad. They
all glared back except Sally Drew, who was simply staring.

"You're the one with gumption," he told her. "Guess you knew
your old pap could take care of himself. You knew he was a
mountain man, was at one time. Never lost, never in the woods.
Some years I lived mostly in them." As a young man he'd spent
a winter in upper Michigan, where it was so cold he and his
bunkmates flipped coins all day to see who would have to get
up and stoke the fire.

"Colin." Daddy spoke toward where he'd moved his lawn
chair out of the light. His tone was calmer now, steadying itself
for a run in the night, against the dark, funneling up and down
through the oaks and the silence that could seize them. "Why
didn't you come when I called you, boy?"

"I've got *some* sense," Colin said, and sounded more animated,
as if affirming it would make it true.

"Some. More than I give you credit for, maybe. A man's got
two daughters. Two chances, and then both chances turn out to
be city boys." He said "city boys" with the precision of a certified
breeder culling the litter.

Colin laughed then. It came out easy, as if he'd readied himself
to play along. "City boys know a thing or two, looks like." The
worst was over, maybe, and his voice was different. He didn't
sound defeated or stubborn but young and virile, the way he
probably thought he looked driving his convertible on the open
highway, speeding to Dallas, one arm across the back of the seat
and touching a woman, even if the woman was his wife.

"How often you walk on something not akin to cement?"
Daddy asked, going for pure country.

"I knew where I was," Colin said. "When you didn't come on

back, I just went to where the car was. No trouble 't'all. Listened to the game awhile—Cowboys knockin' the tar out of the Redskins." He rubbed it in because Daddy lived next to D.C. and was stuck being a Redskin fan, which was a lot like being stuck with your family, nothing he could do about it.

"Why the hell did you start moving the car around?" Tom asked, like maybe he did have some feelings about the afternoon and had been there too. "If you'd just stayed put, Colin."

"I don't know. I moved the car to where it seemed Dad would most likely come out of the woods. Remember, I didn't know what was going on either, so I cruised the road thinking one of you would come along. Sure enough too. You and Becky." It sounded as if Colin might start glaring at Daddy again.

Tom stretched out his legs, deciding to settle in and go along with being part of what happened. "Becky and I never got too far off the road. I was afraid we'd get lost for real and I knew I'd never been lost in the woods before. Hardly been in the woods before. We swam a bit longer, took awhile drying off, and then we waited around the clearing where the car had been. Thinking one of you would be back any minute. I figured you'd gone for a drink of something. It was hot out there. I was thirsty. But as time went on, I didn't know what to think. Started to doubt myself. Thought maybe I was hanging around in the wrong clearing. We went out onto the road then. Becky was starting to heat up and I got a little p.o.'d too, didn't even have anything to read. About the time we were really getting miserable I saw you for the first time, Dad. Skulking behind those trees."

"I saw you before you saw me," Daddy said.

Colin got excited now and jumped up. "Folks, you ain't gonna believe this. A grown man. Grandfather. Defense analyst. Lost in the woods, he comes upon his family at last. He's found. But will he simply walk on out and say howdy? No, his notion of things is to start whooping like a savage and dash around without a stitch."

Daddy got up fast and they thought he might sock one of the boys, but he began to walk back and forth between the light and the dark, sometimes his face showing plainly, and then turned away as if he wanted to hide again, then rush out when they were least expecting it. "I still had my clothes then," he said, and sat down.

"Well, I would hope so," Mamma said, and the women got up to carry the food and dishes back into the house. Tom went to check on Becky, and Colin sat where he was, whistling "The Yellow Rose of Texas," as though he could summon the Alamo.

Daddy let him finish and called the women to come back out and hear the rest of the story, hear about him being lost. "And bring me my whiskey."

That brought Mamma out on the porch, to hush Daddy talking loud through the neighborhood about his drink. Several of those bottomland dwellers rode to Washington in Daddy's carpool. "We're doing the dishes," she scolded him.

"Hang that. You've got to hear. Why else is there any point in doing anything," he added, gazing around at the world and sky.

Mamma and the two daughters were out momentarily, in their aprons and arranged on the picnic bench in a row. Tom and Colin stayed in lawn chairs out of the light. Daddy poured out whiskey for himself and there were extra glasses, but Colin and Tom didn't make a move and nobody encouraged them.

"Today I went into the woods. Took my two sons-in-law and my little grandchild and entered the forest primeval, which is a joke, since we destroyed every remnant of the real thing. I guess to show that we could. No woods anymore is like those I remember back home. Know they were like here, once. But there's some hickory in there, oak to maybe forty feet, a possum or two, whippoorwills at dusk. I like to swim in that quarry. It's deep, cold, and clean. Clean to maybe three hundred feet." He smoked awhile and drank from his glass, everyone waiting for him to go on, waiting to hear about clear water and the old high trees of home.

"We went in there, me scout leading the troops. Tom here tripping on every root and starting to overheat, talking my ear off. Colin yakking about a Coke and did we know the score. That little girl tired out before we left the car."

"She's only four," Marie said.

"She was the least of it. It was those grown men I couldn't take. Smart enough, steady. But there's not an iota of true wanting or anything like fortitude to divide between them." Daddy had drifted away into the dark, but before anyone could get in gear to talk back, he returned to the circle of light as though the curtain had lifted for Scene 2.

"It came to me, heaven-sent. What I wouldn't give to lose that Lone Ranger in the woods. Maybe he'd get to the point of really needing a Coke, not just wanting one and whining about it. I got to thinking he probably hadn't ever been really thirsty in his whole mollycoddled life. Didn't know the first thing about it— standing on a hay wagon stacking bales at a hundred degrees, sucking chaff with every breath. And"—Daddy turned and spoke directly to Colin—"that trick last week at the lake. Holding my daughter here under water."

They'd all been there. Colin and Sally Drew had stood in the shallows splashing each other, dodging and laughing. Then Colin's glasses slipped off, and while he was fumbling for them on the bottom, she gave the water a fillip that sent some smack in his eyes. Made him have to fumble a little longer to find his glasses. When he had them and stood up straight, his face with the jaw set was like the weighting of a proper fraction. He swam out after Sally Drew, who had escaped to the ropes, yanked her to him, and held her under water such a long time, and with such a face, Mamma actually got up and walked near to the water. Daddy began to swim toward them fast, by which time Sally Drew was up, gasping for air and gagging while Colin banged her on the back, the expression on her face mostly puzzled while the blur of water cleared. Without a word, Daddy headed for shore and lay down facing the parking lot, and nothing had been said about it, not until now.

Mamma spoke to Daddy: "You pushed me under that time at Lakeland. Remember? I've been afraid to go in the water ever since." It was a refrain, something she mentioned every time, the wound unrelieved. The others realized they'd been waiting for her, knowing she'd say it, and they were grateful too, Colin off the hot seat, lost in the dark.

"Yes, I recall that event of nineteen hundred and forty, my dear. I've apologized for the last time. Back to today. A fellow like our Tom isn't really that much fun. He's not a lick tougher than Colin, only he doesn't have the imagination to want to be or pretend. It's no matter to him. He'd just as soon pass an hour or two in the woods as not. Doesn't try to hand-wrestle me or titillate me—joy-riding his fat-ass car. Besides, Tom had the child with him. I decided he could go on for a while the way he is, God love him." The night was staying hot and close, never much breeze in the lowlands headed for the tracks. The humidity and the heavy meal added to their lethargy, and they let Daddy take his liberties, caught in the run of his voice, waiting for what came next.

But Colin took up then. He had stories to tell. "In fact," he said, "I lost my shirt once too. In a manner of speaking. Put money in Teleconnections. If it hadn't been for Big John, who put me on to Tower Enterprises, I don't know what might have happened." That was a sore subject with Daddy and they could hear Colin grinning about his Dallas broker, before he went back to the day they'd had. "You asked me to come on with you a little farther. Saying we'd explore while Tom and Becky were swimming." Colin's voice was low and they could hear Daddy beckoning, see the path winding into the dappled woods. "What I want to know—are there really falls in there or was that just part of the damn-fool thing?"

"You'll never know." Maybe Daddy had gone to Big John on

the side and had his own deals, was going to be a rich man too. "One thing I did know for certain, you'd want to show me what a Daniel Boone you are. What I don't figure is how you didn't get any more lost than that. And I did." Daddy sputtered a laugh for the first time since he'd come out of the woods, scratched up and nearly naked.

"Henry. You lose my sons in the forest, or try to. You're late for my dinner that took us the afternoon to fix, those beans from down home. Then you sit there howling. When you were nearly fixed for good." Mamma looked as if she was about to smile in spite of herself, the way she did when she found out the redbird she'd been watching for a week was a cloth one Daddy had perched in the plum tree at the end of the yard.

" 'For good' was about it. But no such luck, my dear. Here I am again." In Daddy's silence was all that he might have gone on to tell her: the sons weren't hers, nor the daughters who belonged to the sons now, the deed to the house in Daddy's name—and certainly not he, who wasn't anybody's. Further, she was pretty much a fool to think anybody ever belonged to anybody. With a sigh he did say, "Can't you tell yet when I'm ashamed?"

That took the wind out of Mamma's sails and she demurred, her voice faint. "You were never ashamed in your life."

"Today I was. I started out to ditch the Texas rider and the fool I lost was myself. In that scrubby little stand of second-growth timber we're calling the woods. There I was, completely alone; Colin vanished without a trace. Didn't hear me when I called." Daddy was out of the light and his voice was mournful, the way it must have sounded, calling with no one to hear.

"But, Dad, I must have seen you after that." Tom went in and out of paying attention, fraying out the mesh on the lawn chair, yawning. It was Daddy's story.

"You did. That was only the first time I was lost and it didn't last long. As I say, we were only about a mile from a telephone or a Coca-Cola. I blundered along calling Colin, couldn't find the path. Already I was leaning on a staff like some old Moses. But then you, Tom, and Becky were there on the road before me and I got to thinking I must look pretty fierce with that stick, scratched up, my shirt ripped, hair mean as Samson. I sneaked up and gave you my hyena laugh."

"A little girl." Marie shook her head.

"She wasn't scared," Tom told her. "In fact, she seemed to know it was Dad right off. Gave me this grin. 'Pappy?' I thought the same thing."

"I know my baby came home crying."

"You both jumped pretty good, I noticed." Daddy was laughing again.

"I mean, right after we knew. Becky even saw you once. 'Pappy's hiding,' she told me. Like you hide in the yard."

"I did get the impression no one was petrified. But I was still aching to sneak up on that cowboy. On my way back to where I thought I'd catch up to him, I smeared my face with clay and poked some twigs in my hair. I wanted to see him when he met up with a real live redskin. Let him yak his way out of that! But I couldn't raise a trace of him, and after a bit I was wondering just which way the quarry might be. The sun was like a boil overhead." His voice was nearly lost over by the back porch and then he was going up the stairs and inside.

Mamma said, "You know, he loves to scare people. Remember how he used to take you girls out on a walk and then run off, leaving you by yourselves? Your aunt says when they were kids he was always waiting in the dark when she went in a room. All her hair fell out once." In the dark no one could see Mamma's eyes, but they recalled them, green as smartweed.

"You better keep an eye out." Daddy was back, the ice rattling in his glass. "First time lost, really lost. It didn't seem hardly possible."

"I've told you, Henry. You're too old to be running through

the woods like a savage. You have a nice yard at home." Mamma loved having the picnic table and benches arranged on the square of brick paving, her roses planted along the side of the house where they got the morning sun.

"Perhaps you're right, after all. Never thought it before. I've traversed every copse inside Butler and Phillips Counties, and if I was perplexed one moment, I recovered the next. I've about lost heart. Maybe I've lived outside this blame city too long, twenty miserable years, and it's always pressing in on me. I figure by now it's about flattened me into a city boy." The defeat in his voice could have been what prompted Mamma to call up his old worn-down dream when she said, "You should have stayed on the farm, Henry. Nothing else ever satisfied you."

That sympathy and generosity, compounded out of resignation, the dim hope of an understanding briefly proffered—Daddy felt ashamed, as though he'd been begging, and answered, "Neither did that at the time." He glared around as if the whole of the world wouldn't satisfy him, not on a bet, raising a cigarette to smoke.

"I lay down, tired out, hot and plain disgusted. When a man can't tell north from south he's finished. Nothing can save him. I collapsed in a stew of pine needles, wrappers, beer cans, glass shards. Filth of every description. Folded my hands and prepared myself. But when I shut my eyes I could smell something faintly woodsy and it took me back. Lulled me so maybe I dozed. When I looked up again the sun was lower in the trees. At least then I knew the way west. But it was all so lonesome, pitiful, and ruined. I thought I might really have died and was getting what I deserved. Listening then, I heard running water and I knew I was found."

"A man don't lay on the ground in Texas," Colin said.

Sally Drew spoke: "Remember the time you killed the rattler, Daddy?" They'd measured it out on the stoop and she'd wanted to have the skin for a belt, only Daddy put it in the garbage and it was gone before she knew. "You said you got its head right under your heel."

"That trail beyond Richie. Dead Man's Knob. Couldn't do it now. Just let it go on and bite me." Daddy's stringy long legs looked as quick and strong.

"You're even chicken to ride with me in my car." Colin had the sense to work that over with a smile.

"Any fool can step on a lever," Daddy said, and they saw his eyes glitter even in that light. Sally Drew reached out to put Colin's arm around her where she'd wanted to wear a snakeskin, but he pulled back. Fixed on Daddy as if one day he'd figure him just right and then they'd ride into the sunset clapping each other on the back.

"In a way I was at peace. I knew it was only a question of time until they'd come to clear for a parking lot or a highway— that reduced, sorry refuge from the bulldozer. I could just lie there and wait." They knew that now he would talk about Uncle Ray's place, the old farm. He was at the headspring.

"One place they'll never get is Uncle Ray's. Way up there on that precipice where he somehow made a living off of hogs and soybeans. A by-God beautiful spot. Ravines, thickets of wild grape and woodbine. There were these high red pines, remote glades that might have seen time begin. All the while the wind sighing on the ridges, sounding like a great rush of water. Blowing and pining. There was a wild man that went with the place too. When I was a boy. He'd be gone now, but it used to be every now and then you'd see him. Like something you felt you might have earned."

"Like a snake," said Sally Drew.

"Mostly you didn't see him, but you'd come onto traces of him, things he'd dragged up there and left. I suppose he'd lost his grip."

"Why wouldn't Uncle Ray have had him locked up?" Mamma asked. "That was a lovely place."

"The old fellow never disturbed it much. It was more a surprise, walking along and then under a clump of bittersweet
there'd be a rubber tire maybe. Attached to a rusted bike. A
heap of broken china, a pink slip, or a lady's pocketbook. I guess
he couldn't help himself."

Tom said he sounded like the first litterbug, but Daddy ignored
him, staring off. His silence accused them all of being irredeem-
ably human, born to suffer and die, lie and hope.

He went on then. "One time I went out to see if I could find
him. Stood all day at the spring house on the edge of the woods
where sometimes he'd come along. Far past noontime when the
apples I'd eaten were gnawing my insides and I was fixing to
leave. Seemed useless and silly. I glanced off into the sky as I
turned, no sun to set that evening, yet the air had that clarity,
a precise quality it gets sometimes in late November, so the woods
stand out, each tree single, the hollow going on with the creek
around the bend—there he was." Daddy stepped into the light.

"Crazy son-of-a-bitch," Colin went off like the report of a
gun.

"He nodded, sober as if we'd met in town. Then he turned
and went on down through the hollow, up the side of the ravine,
and I could watch him a long way in his black coat, the air
purple around him. I knew nothing would ever touch him, no
more than if he was a tree. He never harmed a soul."

Daddy poured from the bottle. The fair hair on his chest
rippled in the light. They heard Bowers going to bed, whistling
in the dog, rolling the shade on the porch, the roller squeaking.
If your neighbors were on you thick as thieves: amuse them,
shock them, drive them nuts. That was Daddy's advice. The
clouds advanced before the moon in their radiance, as if they
did not drift by chance but formed a procession across heaven.

"I thought about the old guy when I was lying on the ground,
and an urge came over me. That was when I decided to leave
my pants and shirt."

"You left them. On purpose. For no reason, on account of some old tramp." Mamma did what she could with that in silence before she added, "If you don't want your clothes, Henry, I think you could at least give them to somebody who needs them."

Daddy didn't answer right off. They all kept quiet and waited for it to pass, hoped that maybe he'd hardly heard, his mind so fixed on what he was trying to say. "My shirt and trousers looked pretty pitiful, I admit, draped on the ground among the Kleenex scraps and cellophane. I added my socks. Not much of a gesture, but I knew I'd never make it back to my loved ones without my trunks and shoes. It was just a sorry little heap, looking more lost than left." He sat down at the table.

"Crazy old tramp." Colin got up and stretched himself, said he was dry as sand and went in the house, turning on the *Late Show*, making the world's noisiest Coke, exploding the ice cubes, clinking bottles, making it clear he was at home whether anyone liked it or not. Once, when he didn't want to eat one of Mamma's country meals of just corn and tomatoes, he went out and bought himself a can of Spanish rice with red meat and heated it up on the stove, ate it out of the pan as if he was starved. The hubbub of guns and stampedes soared into the night.

"Home safe and sound," Mamma finished up, sounding satisfied now that everything had been told and maybe she could get back to her kitchen. Daddy was hanging down between his legs as if he might turn a somersault off the bench or make a running start somewhere. Tom got up too, said he was exhausted, and if Dad didn't mind he'd help himself to whiskey. As he walked over the grass beside Mamma, his shoulders were weighted down so that he didn't look much taller than she was.

Sally Drew and Marie sat where they were in the dark. It was pitch black because Mamma had clicked off the outside light when she went inside. While she straightened up the kitchen, Colin leaned in the doorway, talking loud over the TV, getting a kick out of Daddy's trick backfiring. Him losing himself and

his shirt—the way he was always losing it. For instance buying
the white-painted brick house at the bottom of a watershed,
water pouring into the family room after every little sprinkle.
They heard Tom say he was going to go up and lie in the bathtub,
if nobody minded. Try to relax and get some reading done. He
said he would never own any kind of house. No yard work or
sewer troubles—call the super. Mamma said that you never knew
who it was you married, no matter how long you dated the
person, or even lived together. It sounded in her voice that this
was still a mystifying problem that she would never stop trying
to resolve, though there was no hope at all.

Out in the dark, overhearing or not, Daddy wasn't offering a
word, smoking, grinding his butts under his heel, poisoning the
grass. The kitchen light snapped off and the two daughters got
up and said good night, going to follow their husbands to bed.
Mamma hadn't come to call them, but it was evident from the
way she yanked down the window shade and double-flipped the
kitchen light that she was ready for bed and thought they ought
to be too. From the porch, they looked back to see if Daddy was
coming, but there was no sign of him, no movement at all against
the tracery of moon shadow on the grass imported from the
steppes of Asia. When they turned on the flood again to see more
clearly, there was only the clever little puddle of darkness his
trunks made on the brick pavement surrounding the picnic table.

Peach

THE SEVENTH-GRADE CLASSROOM, rimed in chalk dust, held
like a vibrant shell the chorus of greeting the teacher conducted
while I stumbled toward the desk she pointed out, going by feel—
an awkward oversized girl, new to this school, as I had been new
to so many. This place was only a little less strange, because my
grandparents lived in a nearby town and my mother wanted to
be close to them while my father worked in another state. The
school was in the country, equidistant from several different
towns, a former one-room schoolhouse which had been added
on to and partially modernized. In this room the desks were still
bolted to the floor through an iron stand.

All morning I sat with my face shielded by my elbow-propped
hand, until around lunchtime a boy I didn't see whispered to
someone, "Why's she doing that?" and a bold, not girlish but
definitely feminine voice retorted, "Because she's a dope." After
I recovered from a suffusing flush, I ventured a peek across the
aisle and met a gaze, level and incorruptible, of an absolute and
devastating sincerity, sufficient to determine me never to look
that way again.

She still arrests the eye of my mind, which I imagine is dark and fixed in sober regard, also without remorse or hope. Her eyes, though, looking out, were that singular blue of spring flowers blooming from frost, bluets and forget-me-nots. Their contrast with her long black hair was striking, the native dip and expanse of curl filling it with a glancing light. When we were older and in high school, she probably used rag ends and brush curlers to make some order of it, but when I knew her, when I was twelve, it swept off across her shoulders and in humid weather blew up like a storm cloud frilled with light.

We other girls became her open followers. Not that she didn't have attention from everybody else. The boys included her as one of their own and mothers shook their heads; pursing their lips, they used her as an example. We'd see, they nodded, meaning that fate would be there to hand over the lot inevitably due the heedless, headstrong girl who, unmindful of warnings, would pay. Pay with babies and the consequent ne'er-do-well husband. He would be resentful and, when frustration and drink gave him the excuse, would run with women and generally act the fool. She'd be lucky if he wasn't mean. But we couldn't help ourselves, not then, when everything was being transformed and we needed someone to show us the way. Certainly not some grim-faced, righteous, and disappointed mother.

I imagine it was the women of her family who bestowed the early nickname Peaches an' Cream, shortened to Peach, in unabashed admiration for the gold-flecked cheek of the little blue-eyed girl. There might have been an older sister who, loving her to distraction, heightened the glow natural to her skin with fierce love pinches that nipped it fine. Being the child she was, she sprang, kicking at her tormentor, who dodged and snickered and pinched again. It would have seemed a shame to call her, simply, Faith, her given name.

When I first joined that class, the boys weren't pinching her yet, although they soon would try, concealing ache and rash. It was already in their eyes. But they were hesitant. They learned better than to chase her down in some recess game—boys chase the girls—then deliberately pin her to the ground, for once indifferent to winning, rubbing against her some toady, annealing part of themselves. She would have beaten the shit out of them, taken revenge somehow. There were rumors of older brothers, off at high school or working. The boys were waiting, though, hoping against hope, resorting to prayers in the night. Fuckers.

From her mouth I first heard that word, in that long-ago time, time long like the time it takes for a windbreak of cedars to grow and do some good against both rain and snow when they're wind-driven. I took it to my mother, trembling with anticipation—What does it mean, Mother, dear to me.

"Never. You must never," she panted. Soap and water would not avail, filth, decay, life in the tomb, rats on the gnaw. She slumped, a stricken woman, and I had brought it to her on my tongue. From the next room, where she went to lie on the bed, I heard her hindered breath. I concentrated my vision and sealed the word inside, where it became a jewel studding the eye of my mind. In a twinkling I had become monstrous, and hid my knowing smile.

It wasn't anything to Peach. A shrug and a wisecrack, a dare. A vow that none of it would ever get to her—teachers, boys, ill fortune. Probably it did seem natural enough, came easily out of whatever pig wallow, brat-nasty rabbit hutch spawned her, which, since her mother had died the summer before, didn't offer her even a dependable wardrobe to clothe her rapidly changing form. Already she clerked afternoons at Simpson's General Store, a single dilapidated building at the crossroads going north, pumping gas and selling pop. The next year she went off to high school in another district and vanished. It seemed that way, no word surfacing, and by then no one was interested in looking her up or finding out what she was doing. But at that one-level rectangular country grade school, with its playground and meadowland the only break in the forest's rise and fall, in the classroom that was both seventh and eighth grade, in spring, she brought us to first heat. We stood her between ourselves and a requirement, an exaction we couldn't name but felt in hot pursuit, at the very gates.

Peach did, had always done, whatever the boys did, right along with them, and they expected that sometimes she would beat them at it too and they'd better not grumble or act like bad sports. Not if they wanted to have her with them. In fact, they seemed shy and privileged, maybe on account of the way she'd come to look, and they urged her on, knowing they couldn't scare her or soften her up or work her over to make her sorry or ashamed. "Aw, Peach, come on." They wanted her enough to plead a little, trusting her in that way, knowing her almost since the time when, a drag-diapered wild child, she'd followed her brothers and their friends into the woods, there to do what they told her and not to tell. She didn't either, until the day she refused to go with them, not for that, and they'd respected her for that refusal, accepting her company then as one who was deserving.

The rest of us girls burned with pride that she was still ours and they couldn't touch her, not unless she wanted it, and when she went off with them, they were openly grateful. Little and narrow, though woman-grown, she was willful to the point of arrogance. Had, though it was disguised by lackadaisicalness, an unyielding severity, so like their own that she wouldn't tell who beat up Billy Taylor so that he needed stitches in two places. The teachers, death on a girl who wouldn't tell, shamed her, made her seem almost the one to blame. They passed her over as the helper to collect lunch money or issue library permits. She'd take on anybody. Buck Walters learned that when he laughed at her little sister the time she peed her pants at her desk. But they couldn't dismiss her as a roughneck tomboy either. She was too pretty.

The bus Peach came on was usually the last into the schoolyard, the one bringing in the kids farthest from the school, central to forty miles of townships and farming communities, taking all comers, first grade through eighth. Her bus seemed mostly to carry boys, raw, overgrown country boys. Last and often late, it would sway into the graveled lot and pause, then through the abruptly opened door release such an odd lot of confusion and unpent riot it was as if a herd of unbroken cow ponies had hit the dirt. This astounding exuberance could be capped for book learning only by transforming it into its exact opposite of indolence and hostile indifference. Amid the feverish boys, Peach and a couple of other girls filed off the bus, sedate, with schoolbooks and lunch boxes intact. All those years she had been with them on the long rides of more than an hour, beginning in the dark on rutted dirt roads and in the worst weather, around her the swaggering, the mad-dog talk, curses, and oafishness, amuck in their own vile smells. She probably never squealed or cried out either, disdain mixed with amusement when she wasn't frankly bored. Testing themselves and each other, they watched her while boasting of cockfights, dog fights, bully sessions, not knowing what she might be thinking.

The hounded drivers, no party to any of it, enduring noise and impotence, hunched over the wheel. With their plain wool hunting jackets, necks contracted, ears poking out of raised collars, and lifted shoulders, it appeared the buses were guided by box turtles. There was a driver I heard of who quietly brought his bus to a halt one morning, got out on the side of the road, and walked off. Abandoning everything as he turned his back. Behind him the abruptly silent children stared as he disappeared down the dropping road on his way to the nearest phone, where he called the school and resigned. Retroactive.

Out of that sort of disorder, across long years and miles, Peach arrived each morning at the school door, often after the late bell, and I saw her stand in the doorway, shaking out her hair, sometimes releasing a shower of rain or snow into the air; and into the stuffy overheated room poured a breakneck tang of freedom.

Years before, one teacher had taken a special interest in her. Our teacher mentioned that once, in exasperation, although it did no good and Peach stared back, blank as ever. Perhaps she had summoned that earlier woman to visions of diamonds in the rough, had given meaning to winter hours of stained wool reeking from the cloakroom radiator and the full period allotted to arithmetic given over to investigating the whereabouts of the blackboard erasers. But in that seventh–eighth-grade classroom, Peach shook down her weather-filled hair and fixed on the teacher her blue-eyed stone attention, to learn as little as possible while the class reviewed the state history of New Hampshire and read *The Red Badge of Courage*. She was not obstreperous, unless apathy was so interpreted, and she handed in her papers as if she'd made some attempt to be done with the work or the nagging, if failing to see the use. No doubt they had had their effect, those extended tours with a roving band of miscreants, and must have been part of her mongrelized self-possession. It was contrary to all reason to be delivered to the classroom, hardworking and studious.

I recall myself from that time as tall and thin, though with developed breasts and the anxious, embarrassed expression typical of a girl who has matured too soon. I was very careful about myself so the other girls wouldn't know that I was a full-grown woman masquerading as a child. Part of that was playing dumb about boys and what was referred to as "the facts." I heard them often, recounted by one of the older girls, who had been kept back, and each time I registered surprise and horror, giving her no inkling that her facts differed from what my mother had explained when she read me the book *Growing Up* and told me I had become a woman. I would never forgive her for saying that, as though now I was like her, worried and pinched with woe. In penance for such thoughts, I endured the recitations of my tormentor, who slyly brought the subject round day after day.

It was probably my size that convinced Peach to let me play on her softball team. I could neither hit a ball nor catch one, and most of the time my mind was a million miles away. But I looked as though I ought to be athletic and I presented myself to her, staring at the ground, passively awaiting her judgment. Before that, during recess, I had stood at the side of the school building with another dud or two, but this day I trudged over to where she was forming her team. A ninth player was needed. No one else had volunteered. She looked me over, shrugged, and nodded that I was in, motioning me toward the seven others, girls who'd been in that school with Peach since first grade. Betty Bobbin could really smack a ball and the mastiff-jowled Toots could catch anything that moved. That, in addition to Peach, was the only talent. When she'd picked me for her side, her gaze clouded, resigned. I was the last, although not much better or worse than the others, second-raters.

But we were proud to be on her team, the full nine. When she called us together we squatted in a circle around her, spat off into the dirt, jiggled on our heels, and swore. A skim of moisture fringed her lip and we assumed the resolution of loyal conscripts. Her voice was soft in ferocity, in instruction and oath. After a few words I stopped hearing what she said, my attention always hanging by a thread, wafting away. While she analyzed positions and strategy, my vision blurred. I felt the calling was deeper than that, if thoroughly incomprehensible.

She was already labeled as hard. When girls and their mothers said that, they meant she had hidden herself beyond detection, so that no one could tell what she felt or wanted. But clearly she had feelings. They broke in the sweat on her lip and the skin of her throat splotched with red as full as roses.

"You bitches," she began. We scarcely breathed.

"Yeah, bitches," Betty, the co-captain, seconded.

Sunk deeper than language, I perceived the undercurrent of frenzy which, like all things spiritual and exacting, I bent to serve, forgetful of my own being as though my desires had been subsumed. I would have followed her to war or begun a pilgrimage. Closer to home, in the spring, we attempted softball, pale new leaves shaking, early wood-blooms as frail as morning ice, while overhead the sky sped by on the four winds.

Twice a day we practiced for the twenty minutes of recess, those last recesses of our lives before organized gym classes took their place. Our lunches we took out to the playing field, wolfing the food as we walked along, finishing with a gulp, to take our positions. Noontime was the longest and most important practice, because after school Peach went to her job at the store and the rest of us had the ride home. Most buses were lined up even before the dismissal bell rang, the drivers eager to get it over with. I never knew how Peach got home, but probably there was at least one beat-up jalopy in her yard and some mother's son to hell it down the road. We scraped our own diamond out of the meadow, put down boards to mark the bases in imitation of the regular field, where the boys played. There wasn't enough time in the world, but Peach used what she had, as if she hoped. Although her damp face with its clamped jaw held another look mostly, the hope flickering over her cheek rapidly, like the shadow of a rainbow during a storm.

"A hundred," she demanded. "You miss one, the count starts over." She threw to me herself a couple of times and I began to improve, or thought so. But she knew I would never be good, no matter if I was better. I would always be afraid of the ball, and if that wasn't the last time in my life when I had anything to do with baseball, it would be nearly that.

"Monroe, you're for shit," she snarled once. I felt more exhilarated than offended, happy that she knew my name, called into a new existence where I was ordered about in a code made harsh for intimates. For the two weeks my mother was away on a trip, I wore blue jeans to school, like Peach did, let my hair hang loose, and for perhaps the only time in my life, when I looked in the mirror, found myself beautiful.

Sometimes we'd hear a whistle from somewhere and look up, each of us ready to respond. "When I want *dogs* I whistle." Peach's eyes were bitter. When she wanted our attention, she sent Betty across the field to deliver the message, as if she might have torn out our eyes. "Bitches, whores," she muttered from home plate. After those outpourings she fell into silence, into such a refusal to speak I fancied her rantings had been extraordinary, that she had favored us.

"What do you think we're doing here? Playing house? You'll wish you were dead. Ten times around the bases. Move, goddamn it!" Some boys would pass, stop to smirk, yell out something wise. "Outta here," Peach sneered sidelong, not bothering to look up. When Will Bowles razzed Penny Shoubaugh, she screeched, "Go play with yourself."

Strenuous and noisy, our practice was occasionally fabulous. Or seemed so to me from my station in the outer space of left or right field, which I left for only brief, disappointing turns at bat. Far from me, forms leaped in the air, voices cracked. I paid what attention I could in the noon shimmer. Behind me in the woods, pools of quicksand sucked, exhaling a chill of frozen breath on my neck, and suddenly I would be aware of the faithless moments of departure.

The ball was struck and the sound of the team reached me. "Christ." Betty came near, moving into my domain while the ball landed somewhere around me on the grass. Blinded, I dove in that direction, but it was too late. Betty scooped the ball and made the throw, leaving me without a backward look.

I wanted to do better, but all the time there was that sense of doom inside, which couldn't be managed, and helpless, I suspected my betrayal was imminent. The sun netted in my hair, in a million lateral threads, and it seemed I could smell myself on fire. Only the hoarse cries of my teammates would eventually rouse me. I'd see the ball appear from the heavens and display my glove like an offering, imagining my redemption.

Peach bit herself. In arithmetic I had glimpsed the indented bracelet of teeth marks on her wrist and later I heard the others whisper about it. It was entrancing, shamed us, and made us glad. To me, watching her cramped left hand crawl over the page, showering pencil marks downward, the visible occlusion of her teeth seemed to be winking in a perverse and unacknowledged gaiety. It seemed madness that she was with us, that we could touch her like that, as if the gauze of her hair dropping like a veil over her bent face obscured the heightened passions of a bride. While we, her players, fumbled and blundered, misjudged foul balls with ever more exhilaration, wordlessly she sank her teeth into her own flesh.

Ted Shannon was the captain of the boys' team and sometimes at noon he came over to watch us awhile. He didn't gloat or flirt, just watching, and one day after he'd seen Peach take the mound and then her turn at bat, he went up and asked if she'd like to play on his team. He asked in front of everyone, his eyes squinting and serious under his beaked cap, not seeming to notice at all that there were blue eyes so cold and crystalline it was as though they would never see summer. She didn't huff around or get haughty with Ted, only refused him, man to man, explaining that she had her own team. Disappointed, he asked her who she thought we would be playing anyway, but Peach only shrugged.

Ted didn't ask again, but he'd watch her sometimes from where his team practiced, and then we heard that the second-grade teacher, who was the coach, yelled at him in front of all the guys, "Ted, or maybe I should call you 'Tiddy,' if you don't quit eyeing the girls. See if they'll let you jump rope."

That stopped him, but I didn't think it was because he cared about being called a sissy; it was more that he didn't want to let his own team down. I had worked in the school cafeteria, where his mother cooked, and I could tell from the way she talked about Ted that he was the kind of boy who made a mother proud, that he had principles and thought it was honor and truth that made a man. Sitting in the seat behind him that spring I could see how carefully he completed his exercises before he'd turn around to tease me for being only half done, and he didn't seem to care who saw him cry the day they had to take Harvey Boar to the children's home. While I contemplated the year's weather, hazy sometimes and then clear as summer's evening light, moving over Ted's neck, the skin at the nape delicate as a moccasin flower, he was advancing toward being the man he was destined to be. I could feel it blazing in him, the intent and wonder of it, could see it in his eyes when he'd finish up and turn around in his seat.

"Catch anything yet?" He grinned into my eyes, sharing my misgivings, doubts, and self-mockery. He might become serious then, for a second. "You oughta pay more attention. Concentrate. That's the only way to get better." Then he'd go back to his work, go on building his character. Seventh-grade arithmetic was like second grade's, only the columns were ten times longer, featuring sevens and nines. Ted worked at them steadily, adding up and checking down, the only one of the boys who got them all right, just as sometimes I was the only girl who got them all wrong. Except for Patty Foulks, who didn't try and was fifteen just staying in school until she could quit. She didn't even attempt the problems but copied them out in perfectly formed numerals, so minute as to be nearly illegible. Then she folded her hands on top of her paper in the attitude of prayer, as though that was her last resort, in which she had complete confidence. I wondered what was wrong with her. She didn't open her mouth in class, took the zero instead. But her mouth didn't hang slack, her eyes were clear, and when her name was called she looked up, blushing. It puzzled me why anyone would drag together the two gap ends of a large hole with a safety pin, in plain sight. Under and around the pin I glimpsed the soiled pink of her brassiere, her white skin. When the boys snickered openly about her "tits," Patty's silence thickened, but she never changed clothes or mended what she wore, just as she never even tried to add two and two. There were times when such wondering kept me from doing a single problem, but I wasn't failing like Patty, because other times I got them all right.

"Goddamn," Peach said when Bernice Oneacre had to go home at noontime because her mother had a new baby. Bernice flushed but she had to go. Her mother needed her. "Babies." Besides scorn there was accusation in Peach's tone, as if with an unknown power she had discerned contemptible longings in all of us. "Yeah," we chorused. "I'd rather be dead," she interrupted. "Play ball!"

I wandered off to my position in left field. It was a cool day, the gusting wind lifting up the dirt which was just loosened from frost, the trees silently fluttering, leaves still tiny. Dirt gritted in my eyes, and was partly what made me miss the ball, in spite of my energetic attempt to field it, running in circles and groveling on my knees. When I had it, I raised my eyes to see where to return it and met Peach's gaze. Charging the ether between us, it was tangible and reflected light like an instrument for precise measurement. Almost imperceptible, a nod from her moved Betty across the field in my direction. This time Peach came behind her. They made the long walk slowly, passing through the discrete figure of the diamond while I waited. Then they took me by my arms and led me, limp and unresisting, though stumbling a time or two, up through the field to home plate. All the girls were watching from their stations and it was as though the whole world chastened me when Peach brought her hand up and across my face with a sharp slap. My teeth rattled, the light branched razzle-dazzle. I dropped my head forward and a tear I didn't know was there fell on my shoe.

"Nothing personal," she said. "From now on, anybody goofs, they get the works."

Two more girls were punished that noon. When I went inside I found an apple sitting on my desk for everyone to see. It had been highly polished and glowed with an aura. I covered my face

with my hand and sat all afternoon that way, left without touching the apple. The next morning it was gone. None of us girls
who had been slapped said anything or acknowledged each other
in any way, either that day or any of the days following, when
it became quite regular. After a while the punishment was so
automatic and undisputed it seemed like an element in a ritual
observance, vested with a significance beyond common understanding. Finally we played worse than ever, until we could do
nothing right, enduring a radical, ineffectual consequence that
seemed increasingly ludicrous.

We were doing arithmetic one afternoon when the teacher
called Patty Foulks to the board. We were all called up, in groups
of four, and it was just Patty's turn and I didn't think to look
up, already knowing her few disrepaired clothes, her greasy hair
that wasn't washed from week to week, so that she was one of
the first checked for head lice when the county nurse came to
school. It took the silence going on extra long in the ebbless
tension of an inheld breath for me to realize something had
happened, and I looked up, together with the teacher, who raised
her eyes as her lips said 977. Her dismay swept across her face
in a solid wave, and with identical speed she went to Patty,
whispered in her ear, and then walked with her to the door.
Patty, although she knew what was wrong, did nothing to conceal
the dark stain spreading on the back of her skirt, her face as
pale as though all her blood had been drawn. Her eyes stared
with the repudiation of a drowned idol which regards the eternal
darkness from the bottom of a lake. The silence in the room
after she'd gone kept the quality of surpassing stupidity, and
not one boy smirked. Patty did not return to the classroom, and
the next morning, her desk was already cleared out. Empty in
the center of the room, it seemed, because of the sudden and
unmentionable vacancy, that she had been banished.

The teacher begged for attention all through the hours before
lunch, although there was little commotion, just a continual

distraction. Then at noon the girls didn't walk to the diamond but milled and straggled around by the building, kicking stones and muttering among themselves. Someone said, "There ain't even nobody to play." Three of them finally appointed themselves to go to Peach and announce that they were going to skip practice that day and watch the boys' game, which would begin right after lunch, the first real game with another school. I came close in time to hear Peach say, with a fling of her head and that predictable unflagging remoteness, "It's a free country."

The girls shrugged and backed off, then turned and bolted for the other field. "Meet you after," Betty called as she followed, and there, in her voice and in their rush, something relaxed, stretched taut and then released, so they were already laughing as they ran. I stayed with Peach, feeling the girls like a cord pulling at me from beyond, until she got up and walked into the school.

Ted Shannon was on the mound when I got there. In full sun his hair glowed reddish, and hot, it had the texture of corn silk, damp-furled at his brow. His face and arms glistened and throbbing veins seemed to bind him in live rope. He had passed beyond the ordinary attachments of this life, his forgotten self attending a single flame. He existed within a strict preordained process, time absorbed into the progression of event. In the way he played ball I saw how he would do all important things.

The game went on, the away team striding to bat and then our team. Seven innings went by until long past noon. I rarely saw the ball, lost in the roar going on around me. When occasionally I would hear the whack of a bat it resounded as a lone clear note in music, suggesting theme and order. Around me the girls cracked their gum and clutched each other in excitement. "Did ya see him nab that one? Ain't he the one. My cousin goes to his school. Bet she knows him."

Buck Walters, after he struck out, threw the bat and then his cap on the ground, wiping his red face with an arm as he dragged toward the bench. Ted Shannon swatted his behind and some of the others threw an arm around his shoulders. The girls stirred and Becky McVearry passed down her rabbit's foot. He stuffed it in his pocket without looking up.

When the game was over, our boys made a circle with their arms thrown around each other and, stubborn-jawed, followed Ted's example and forced themselves to be good sports and cheer the winning team. The bus pulled away with the team from Sunderland, and leaving, they leaned out the windows and banged at the sides. Safe now, they teased the girls, begging to meet them on Saturday at the picture show. "Hey, good-looking. Give us a kiss." Daredevil strangers, spurred on by the visible offense to our own sulking boys.

The girls disappeared back into the school, ignoring Peach and their promise to meet her. I went over and sat with her, not saying anything when she didn't look up. Against the edges of the diamond the fresh-scuffed lime puffed in the breeze. I was rehearsing an oath of loyalty, a pledge to suffer humiliation, to hunt to the death the things that are extreme and pure, that resist inclusion, when Peach stood up and started toward the highway. She was probably headed for work, but I tagged along at a distance, uninvited. I wasn't sure she knew I was there until she stopped at the pavement and turned, waiting for me to hurdle the drainage ditch.

Her eyes stared over my shoulder. "You were getting good too," gulping with the lie. "Wait till *they* get the curse." Her dry lips were whitened at the corners as if dabbed with lime.

My mother was waiting at the door when I reached home, disturbed after the school called that I'd left early without permission. I pushed on past her and locked myself in the bathroom. She heard me crying and banged on the door, ordering me to open up. I nearly checked for spots before I began to calm down. Somehow Peach had guessed about me and now I knew she was a woman too. I must have seemed really ill when I opened the door, for my mother put her arms around me and took me to bed.

On Monday, when I returned to school, it was as though I was the new girl all over again. The teacher, making good her threats from the week before, had assigned us different desks over the weekend and I was placed among strangers, far from the group I'd sat with before. At noon the girls, as though by prearrangement, took their sandwiches and went to watch the boys practice. Some of them started leading cheers, and nobody mentioned the girls' team. I spent those last lunchtimes that year eating alone at my desk, reading as fast as I ate, with the goal of finishing a book a day.

After that, Peach went around to watch the boys play sometimes, but more often I glimpsed her smoking out in the driveway with older boys who drove over from the high school. When she was absent from school, I'd see her from the bus when I rode home, pumping gas at the general store. She'd begun to apply an Egyptian-red lipstick I'd seen displayed at the dimestore in town. It made me think of Patty, whose blood had run out in such a quiet way and made us all turn pale.

Ted Shannon got a crush on Peach and they met at the movies. I heard kids say that his mother didn't approve, and he fibbed and said he was doing something else. Sometimes now he was the one who didn't finish his arithmetic on time, and when he looked over my way, his eyes were dreamy, not seeing me. It seemed impossible that I had ever bent forward to catch in my mouth the sunlit motes spinning around his head, that he should have given me an apple brilliant as a jewel. It seemed that an eon had slipped by as quick as a wink.

The next year both Peach and I went away from there, Peach to live with an aunt in another town, and I moved five hundred miles to a different state. In the summers I sometimes went back to visit my grandparents, but none of the girls I met from the high school had ever heard of a girl named Faith—or Peach—

Warren. Ted Shannon was an honor student and captain of the high school's baseball team but he'd never had a girl named Peach. Not that anyone knew about, although it would happen sometimes that when he got in a jam pitching, one of the kids from the old school would call out, "Come on, Ted. You can do it. Come on! Do it for the Peach."

An Energy Crisis

JERRY BENNETT stood at the tip-top of his house for a bird's-eye view. Three stories up, and then beyond the widow's walk, into the branches which overhung the square Victorian edifice, latter period, he was poised and proper as the groom consenting from his wedding cake—minus fifteen to twenty pounds and years. Below him, the gingerbread ornamentation, boat-wheel spindles, posts and pillars, dormers and shutters, festooned the house, trivial and yet necessary to the effect, as frosting makes the cake. This excess decoration, anachronistic and spirited, delighted Jerry, as did his own ebullience, the pearl of adornment upon the analytical and sensible soul he strove to be in the conduct of everyday affairs.

He surveyed the unobstructed view of the mountains to the south while Hazel remained below supervising the movers in their dispatch of the family's possessions, selecting armchair *tête-à-têtes*, whisking children from the paths of washers and stoves freewheeling on dollies. He had swung himself up the attic ladder, along the smooth oak staves ribbing the tower like the hull of a ship, on through the roof hatch to the outside balustrade. The height intoxicated him; he made ready as if to declare—

victory, a jubilee. He called to Hazel on the sidewalk, a speck in the distance. His brown hair ranted, but what he had to say was whirled away in the leaves.

Although they were moving into the old house that day and it was a stolen pleasure, Hazel lingered a moment under the shade of the ancient trees and felt she had come home. She would have neighbors of all ages and types, babies and grandmothers, men who didn't work for the company with Jerry. She imagined them becoming friends, arriving at her parties, bringing her casseroles when she was sick. The house, aged and a bit worn and grayed-out, showed a neglect that was as comfortable and familiar as her own flesh-budded thighs. Its front tower rose up above the roof and bowered in the branches of maples, and a triumphant elm, still alive and flourishing against all odds, dominated the back yard. Hazel went inside again, strengthened and hopeful even in the face of Dutch elm blight and company transfers.

Two months earlier, Jerry had come home from work with the news that the company would be assigning them to upstate New York. Immediately he had described Hazel as the original small-town girl restored to the scene of her girlhood. He had said he would see to it that she lived in a small country village, and had one of those big old houses she'd always wanted, room for a garden. "Now," he'd warned, "some of those hick towns are on the seedy side. No class at all. But with the plant expanding, new folks coming in, we'll have benches on the green in no time. Move in on some of those mom-and-pop operations. Jesus. You wonder how they survive. Not even quaint." His tempo accelerated to include old trees, the sewage-treatment bond issue— the dialectic of progress.

"This plant expansion will be their lifeline," he'd expounded to Hazel, and she, overwhelmed if not fired up by the portentous bellow of his lungs, couldn't object. "Whatever happened to the dam on the Connecticut?" she slipped into a pause, recalling a project he'd touted not long before, but he didn't hear. His former position was rapidly becoming *ex post facto* and Hazel watched her own life swept by on the same tide. Even her determined pleasantries had been subverted into the innuendo and absent-mindedness of an incipient hysteria. Lacking Jerry's force, her issue resembled the sibilant murmur of a brook absorbed into a cataract.

"We can't leave our future, the future of the world, hostage to the whims of desert nomads and camel drivers. We'll outsmart them as they wander in their bedsheets. I've an idea we can push a pipeline right across the Canadian Rockies and bring in the oil. Alaska did it! There's room for energy and antelopes." With Jerry safely launched on the open seas of the international oil embargo, Hazel's mind could drift to consider the logistics of the upcoming move with their four boys. In passing, she gave a parting nod to the fate of the dam project which had occupied Jerry for the previous two years. In an odd way she had become attached to it.

"My dear," Jerry said to Hazel that first night in their village home, several miles from Albany, while she layered shelf paper, stocking the cupboards of whitewashed fir, "how would you like the kitchen to be?"

"I love it," she answered, a little off beat, distracted by the dispersion of her children into the bedrooms of the fourteen-room house. She might not have heard Jerry correctly over the crash and tumult of his dreams. Up on the roof he had realized he commanded space, leagues and leagues of living space. It seemed as alive to him as the sea, mute but resistant. Obstacles and procedures absorbed him, blueprints, inventories, materials. Opportunity seized him by the throat and he fell silent.

Or was the stricture a scimitar at the jugular? It was intolerable to Jerry that the Arabs should threaten him, his job and nation. At the plant he would be heading the development of an alter-native energy system for the industry's expansion. He could see further—his plan setting an example for the village, the region, appealing to Yankee traditions of self-reliance. Jerry told Hazel all this and more in a recurring lecture which he augmented in the interlacing and charming style of political and economic arabesque. Not that he blamed the Arabs. Not until sand amounted to something.

A foreign-made bicycle was one of Jerry's early purchases. Its ten speeds were more than he needed for the straight shoot to the plant, he admitted to Hazel. But someday he might go farther, tour the continent. "Join the resistance," he called as he drove away at his pedals and parted from her, heading for the plant that first morning under his own steam.

Hazel watched from the doorway. He entered the highway, hunched over the curved handles, his face crimson with the double strain for breath and her attention. He shouted something she didn't hear. It sounded like "From manifest destiny to the whole earth," something he might have said.

Town water and sewage disposal: Jerry attended village meetings to involve himself and his enlightened management in community affairs. "They still dump their shit in the river, for Christ sake. Cars in the yard. Well, when this house is painted they'll have something to live up to," and he ordered forty gallons of Williamsburg blue. He mustered his four young sons, TV addicts, soon to be drug addicts if somebody didn't take hold, and inaugurated their conversion into the useful and diligent citizens of a bygone era. Newly enthralled by the family unit in principle, he patted himself on the back for creating one. Patted Hazel for her part, describing life as it used to be and the future too; and she thought, listening to him, both were inescapable, just as they were presented.

Jerry assumed very nearly a public obligation. He would restore the exterior of his 1890s home to its former harmony of design and ornamentation. The house had weathered for years; no neighbor recalled its last paint job. "I got you your old house, didn't I?" He nuzzled Hazel and she laid her plump hand in his. "Now I've got to fix it up."

One fall Saturday he rounded up his crew of boys, the youngest still in fuzzy hand-me-down Doctor Dentons, put scrapers in their hands, and, worrying all alike with a harangue of instructions, cautions, and inspiring messages, set them to work. He chided them for their attitude, which he found resentful and withholding, quite unlike that of little boys of yesteryear.

He left for the paint store. An hour later, back with torches, blasters, ladders, and rolls of insulation, he began to work. Paint chips rained on the grass, hammers beat, crowbars tugged. By evening the porch steps sagged in the yard, pillars rested against the side wall, ruined shingles plastered the lawn. Bales of tar paper approached the melting point in the heat of Indian summer. Those erstwhile apprentices had long since deserted, their indolence noted by Jerry, then dismissed. They had been little help, quarrelsome, peeking at cartoons through the window. He would go it alone, not the first to suffer a mutiny.

Entering the house at dark he told Hazel, "Put an Arab on relief—insulate." He told her on and on, until the light was extinguished in their bedroom and she was shuttled between sleep and response: the obscurities of paint specs, of pigments, of rot and powder-dust beetles. Modern children. "But we'll lick them," he exulted, smacking her on the rump to arouse her to an embrace. "We got here just in time," he whispered low.

He'd begun but he couldn't finish. Not in the depths of fall, close to Halloween, when the weather had become too cold for paint to spread and dry. Leaves blew and flailed the shingles, and there was a rush on the north side, to lay tar paper over the exposed insulation before it sailed away, to reset the nails, while the wind surged and open sky among the branches of the single elm expanded. Hazel engaged a tree service to prune and feed the tree, and she and the arborist agreed she had a beauty there, a true survivor.

Jerry struggled on, usually alone, nights and weekends when he could. One sunny day he painted the front tower the authentic blue. "To reassure them," he motioned vaguely to the outstretched town which, perceptibly drowsy, seemed intent on hibernation. His project was ennobled by haste, frozen finger in the dike of winter, though eventually the ladders stood anchored in snow and what could he do? They rose like permanent fixtures, rococo illustrations of trelliswork. The pillars from the front porch listed here and there, and four steps mounted the weeds in the side yard.

Jerry moved indoors. It was high time Hazel had the kitchen she deserved, she his wife who cooked each day for six, for whom he gave his all. This kitchen would stamp out waste, the waste of time and energy routed in a fiberglass, stainless-steel assault. For serenity at mealtime, he fancied an old-fashioned inglenook extended off the far end of the house, one wall a massive fireplace. A thermopane picture window would exhibit the yard and its trees, the rolling foothills beyond.

"You will serve us there," Jerry lured Hazel, envisioning a delightful mixture of oysters and cream, himself at rest, tamping a Turkish mixture into his pipe. The fire will dance as we clink our glasses, his fancy roamed, while aloud he whetted his tongue on the historical and technical evolution of shelter beginning with the cave. Hazel encouraged him there by the iron sink, her hair frizzled in the steamy air. Flour puffed as she worked the bread into loaves. Inspired, Jerry detailed the plumbing system, explicating the interrelationship of traps and vents, his analysis evoking ebb and flow as he gushed his inexhaustible information.

Another Saturday Jerry eliminated the side entrance to the kitchen, cutting a new door into a corner of a south wall, through plaster, double-backed lath, and the outer shingles. The expansion at the plant had suggested this—the laws of thermodynamics demanded it. Such, Jerry confided to Hazel, was the vigilance needed to conserve heat. It was inconvenient for Hazel to lug bags of foodstuffs for six people around the sprawling house to get in the back.

"I'll slim down bringing in the groceries," she laughed to a friend whose husband worked for Jerry. With one crooked finger she wiped laughter's tears from her eyes, careful to preserve the makeup techniques she had mastered many years ago. Once it had been venturesome, the bronze-plate hairdo, the layered fretwork of lashes, a lacquered slice of mouth, although often now it seemed labored, as if the heart of the thing had slipped away. Jerry said she was still the girl she'd always be for him. He said it absently as he pried the pantry cupboards off the wall.

Then winter, the wolf in the larkspur, was on them full force. Jerry identified herbs in the dead garden and concocted vile teas. He stalked the thermometer, caulking the windows tight, searched the heavens for snow. Straining his head toward the Great Bear, he robed his family in the feathers and furs of the creatures. Winter at last; Jerry laboriously stacked a truckload of wood into an ordered stand of two-foot cylindricals. Firm and brown, they satisfied him as though he had made them himself. Prepared, he awaited the Bear and the sheiks of the East, who joined forces against him.

Hazel despaired that her down parka, a birthday present from Jerry, added pounds and years to her appearance. A veil seemed ample protection if there was fire and friends to admire it. She invited neighbors in for a small gathering, a mix of village people and others Jerry knew from the plant. There would be candlelight and wine, no mention of birthdays. In a long dress, with scarves and hooped earrings, sipping her glass of sherry, Hazel greeted them all. In the distance the beat of a hammer. "Where's Jerry?"

Hazel shrugged them onward if they dared, her smile rueful. Some brave ones went to find him, pushing aside the velvet drapes, musty and flabby from years of attic storage, now returned to their original rod over the living-room archway. They ventured on into the dim, unheated reaches of the house. There

Jerry would answer their questions in the fullest detail—she wished them well.

To those remaining with Hazel, sheltered by brown velvet, it was as if they'd lifted the folds of a tent and entered a paradise of fire and incense. Indeed, they'd had to tunnel in the front door under the ladders and posts, assisting each other over the gap to the threshold. Once gaining the house, they felt victorious, abandoning a mound of boots and coats to freeze in the front hall. Hazel in her draperies told fortunes in shy bursts of clairvoyance. "You will, you will." She knew what those people wanted, those people from the plant. None of the villagers, the locals, had come—they might as well be living in Hartford.

The oil shortage restored power to winter, priestly authority to fire. Packed into the overheated room, the guests churned with confession. Mortals, they were aghast before the exactions of the flesh. Their fervor resounded in strains of emotion, the telling of tales. Already that winter old people had frozen to death, huddled around drained oil tanks. Prices had doubled between one delivery and the next. There were rumors of false scarcity, collusion, and black markets. It was a risk to begin any journey, gas stations closing down in whole regions without warning. The men stretched and shifted, awaiting their turn at moist-eyed disclosure. Thermal units, drafts, vacuums, creosote—obscure terms garnished their conversation as the satin-black olives from Arabia trimmed the salad bowl. Among themselves the wives shared their domestic trials and fears, aroused too, but they left the technicalities to those who made their mastery a preoccupation.

Finally Jerry arrived, leading his dazed companions out of the cold. A fresh beer in hand, he seemed primed to divest himself further of everything he had ever known. Hazel's grace with the relish tray evoked the whirl of a dancing girl, until, feeling obligated to join with the others, she leaned against the antique secretary to listen. Abstracted, she lost track of what Jerry was saying in the blare of evensong from the Catholic church, the recorded static of the bells overwhelming wisdom.

"Those who won't adapt will go under," Jerry assured his audience. "Not least those yokels at the corner with their cement-block monstrosity. We'll attract business with some class, craft shops and boutiques. Cram zoning down the gullet, regulate subdivisions, promote land conservation." His color rose, a dilation of veins thickened the heft of his upper lip while his men, his subordinates at the plant, strove to pay their dues as now they settled against the wallpaper and into the corner moldings.

Jerry's tidings absorbed him utterly. He teetered on a logroll of implications, oblivious to his circumstances, gesturing as he bit and chewed, a mélange of food and thought proceeding in and out. For a final treat he herded everyone off to view the wood stove, which now occupied the center of the dining room, the mahogany table and chairs pushed off in the corner. The sheet-metal box was the last word in airtight efficiency—he told them all about it. Alone, Hazel waited in the living room by the window, watching the snow as it fanned and spun, iridescent in the street lamp, before the dark and frigid world which man must heat.

In bed at last, she closed her eyes, laying her cheek beside the mesh fixture of her coiffure while Jerry journeyed on, ascending and descending toward the horizon, a prairie schooner claiming the desert. Hazel slept, but Jerry, in full powers, left the bed for the parlor and began loosening the butternut molding that corniced the tinwork ceiling. In the break while he rested, the branches of the old elm sawed out a high thin note.

Anticipating the contractor, Jerry approached the wall between the kitchen and dining room with a hammer and chisel. When it was demolished and the back wall had been extended, there would be one open space, in accordance with the most contemporary design. In the meantime, the family ate in a corner, facing the wall, sweltering four feet from the "latest in wood

stoves," Jerry's phrase, though hardly an oxymoron when oil
was the equivalent of solid gold. The gaping hole in the plaster
took on a different face day by day and the boys found it made
a convenient tomb for vegetables.

"It's morning," Jerry declared, beginning a winter day, entering the kitchen and briskly rounding the corner to the wood
stove, stretching his arms and uncrimping his vocal cords. "Boy,
it's cold. Did you put wood on the fire? How'd it last the night?"
Rapid-fire interrogation while he brought armloads of wood from
the shed. He grabbed the poker and shovel, wrenching the door
open to battle the drench of sparks and glowing coals that tum-
bled onto the floor, rolling about on the rug. Snatching them as
he could, Jerry shoved more wood in the stove, braced his knee
to force the door. The fracas was accompanied by strenuous
discourse on the procedures vital to wood heat, the subtleties of
damper control. "Did you call George about delivering that
coal?"

"I meant to." Hazel was distracted by the brands newly scarring the hooked rug that had been her mother's.

"I don't care if you meant to. Did you?" Under his scrutiny,
Hazel felt her lip tremble as if she might be in danger of losing
her allowance.

"I will today. But we already have plenty of wood, don't you
think?" She hesitated to ask why they still needed a cellarful of
coal. It seemed excessive, like hoarding gasoline.

"No, I don't think. Hazel, our lives depend on this. It's been
below zero for a goddamn week."

She wasn't following his logic, and something in Jerry's eye
warned her not to mention the furnace and the full tank of oil,
although by the time he was satisfied, it might be hazardous to
strike a match. She nodded her head.

"Good. This house you wanted so much is a real glutton.
You've got to watch it every minute." Forgiving Hazel, Jerry
placed her ear to the draft. She was afraid for her hair under

its spray net, but covered it with her hand, risking immolation to lay her head against the metal and hear the air in the chimney. The wail, streaming up the center of the house, was in one ear. Jerry's disputation and urgency filled the other. Inside, they canceled each other out.

While he ate and shaved, Jerry discussed the advantages of the airtight stove, the threat of chimney fire. He assisted one son with algebra and counseled another on the arcing path of a sidearm pitch, all the time holding his coffee aloft, gesturing wildly. Hazel imagined it signaled distress.

To Hazel it was "Call George," and he was out the door and into the car, off to herd the car pool to the corral at the plant. The ten-speed hung from a sling in the garage. "Bikes will do in a pinch," he'd informed Hazel, "but the one-to-one, person-to-vehicle ratio has had its day."

That evening Jerry came from his labors in the old storeroom he was paneling for an office. He'd heard music in the distance, although it was after eleven. He parted the velvet drape to the living room, as warily as if he was entering a den, disturbed by the hiss of shuffling slippers, tinkling cymbals catching eerie rhythms. Uncharted dunes shifted at his feet, Hazel adrift in violet chiffon. Her stomach, no longer a pillow for his head, undulated and quivered within visible muscle quadrants, bare between the tasseled girdle and bra. Her personality, that thumbed and beleaguered bag of tricks, quickened and retreated in the curve of her lips. When she saw Jerry, she shrugged, with a shy giggle retrieving a bra strap. "Belly dancing," she expirated with the circumambulation of her hips. "Getting in shape." The man, his long-drawn nasal cry on the recording, could have been exalting.

"Next you'll plug up your navel with a ruby." Jerry retreated to his work, as spent as a sultan on his couch. That night he had nothing to say, although in succeeding days he hit his stride, confiding to Hazel his confidence in her innate good sense. He would overlook her consort with the enemy. Not for him to confuse a woman's artistry with betrayal, women's liberation with deceit. He was like a Regulator clock, in its day the last word in time. Hazel ventured a few words about hips, a woman's fears that her body was gross, but Jerry knew better. Belly dancing would pass, and in the meantime he'd be there to help her, keeping the home fires burning while she had her fun.

To her daytime lessons in Middle Eastern dance, as the teacher Sirena called it, Hazel added an evening class at the Y and began to let her hair hang straight in the new style. That evening a week, while Hazel danced, Jerry was left with the children. He advised them on homework, lectured and tested, probing for deficiencies in them and their teachers. Abruptly he would sentence them to extra chores, fitful disciplines, subsequently to early bedtimes and television blackouts. They cried for their mother, drew shaving cream graffiti on the mirrors. Finally off to bed, one child would play favorite, feigning an interest in logical consequences until Jerry came to his senses and carried the sleeping child from his lap to bed, his heart stirred.

"Still working, dear?" Hazel called, coming into the house one evening. She was late and went directly to find Jerry, her round face glossed with cold. She stopped short, a hapless afterthought amid the dismantled stove, sink, and counters where only that afternoon she had prepared shrimp Newburg. Everything familiar seemed to have departed, set loose from the moorings of pipes, plugs, and walls. Hazel grasped at the remnants of her cheerful traditions. "I guess I can cook in the fireplace, wash up in the bathroom."

"It's a matter of contiguous elements, exactitude, getting to the bottom of things," Jerry said, hidden under the counter. "It seemed the right time to move on this, with you gone so much."

"Gone so much" hung in the air, flinty, sounding through the screws and nails studding his mouth.

Jerry appeared from under the U joint, yanking up his trousers.

Then seeing Hazel so fretful, he relented and spoke to her of renovation as concept, of dedication—everything done for her. Dreamlike, a vision of Hazel accompanied his words, Hazel in an apron, oven-rosy, an embossed rolling pin in hand, moonlight on the distant foothills. He would nourish her on discourse, harmony in architecture, function married to design. Absently, Hazel wound the violet veil around her throat.

At the vernal equinox Jerry declared spring, and the contractor arrived with his crew. Hazel began another session at the Y and Jerry acknowledged it was only reasonable. The children were growing older, she needed interests of her own. He thought it conceivable that belly dancing would foster international relations. Hazel watched him sideways—he did not look like a man who had forsaken battle, forgiven enemies, his shaggy hair concentrated in two forward tufts. It was more that he had entered another arena, pursued another foe.

But it was true she couldn't cook much in the kitchen, or spring-clean, with sawdust blowing and the yard mud-packed. Jerry said he dreamed nightly of the time when she returned to her duties. "We'll have to fatten you up." He grinned, pinching at the diminished fullness under her bosom. "I always like a woman with something extra."

"You're the only one," Hazel grumbled, then regretted the implication and added, "But you're the one who counts," avowing their home was a fortress, built upon Yankee pot roast. But Jerry had to declare the kitchen off limits as the addition got under way. He brought dinner home, chicken and hamburgers from the carryouts multiplying along the highway leading from the plant. It occurred to Hazel that nobody else in the modern world really needed to cook.

In the summer it was necessary to rent a cottage for Hazel and the boys. Jerry joined them for brief visits, but usually he went home at night, overseeing the project. He slept in his clothes on a cot in the living room, ready to spring to action, scribbling back-of-the-envelope notes. Hazel sensed rebuke in this arrangement, the growing silences, and when she asked if everything was all right at work, he looked suspicious, as though it was none of her business. He mislaid his keys and scrambled the syntax of his atypically simple sentences. He too was thinner, eating on the run.

It seemed to Hazel that her house had departed on a journey from which it would never return. She mourned, with the unaccountable remorse fastening to spurned loves, the worn maple flooring, porcelain clawed fixtures, tin ceiling medallions, the ribbons twirling over the wallpaper. As irretrievable were Jerry's monologues, the bombastic soliloquies—their destination no longer charted in ceaseless combinations of smoke-like reformations.

By late summer, Jerry, still mysterious and possessive about his plans, hinted that finally the kitchen was large enough and splendid. He began in earnest on other rooms. Why not—while they were at it, this man who had serenaded her though her days, muttering and distracted.

At the cottage, Hazel went on with the life she had made in three rooms and a sleeping porch. She gardened a sandy patch near the beach, gathering a few squashes and string beans which she nibbled sun-warm and raw. The boys pursued their mad games, swam and screeched at waterfront cookouts, then slept where they fell by the burned-down fire. They were happy enough, if bewildered, to be so free, fed hot dogs by a mother who had become indifferent to regular mealtimes, whose laugh was so brief it resembled a sneeze.

Nights, under a dangling light bulb, Hazel began to revive her typing skills, swatting the moths that brushed her face and silted her papers. She talked to an employment agency and began to diet in earnest, further erasing from her face and figure the slack crescents of indulgent maternity.

The world made its faithful turn toward winter as if to demonstrate a better way. Hazel drove the boys to the village school, without detouring to pass the house, returning to the cottage to type forty words a minute, with a hot plate blazing near her ankles. Until the evening when, emerging from the disorder and dementia of restoration, Jerry arrived at the door to give Hazel the grand tour. Just the two of them. He pinned an orchid corsage to her sweatshirt and hurried her toward the car.

When he helped her in, shyly he complimented her manicure, as if he was seeing her polished nails for the first time, although she'd revived the practice early in the summer, as an adjunct to secretarial skills. On the way over, he said he had a surprise, and she gripped the seat, her nails turned to black in the fading light. Across from their house someone had a sign out, TROPICAL FISH FOR SALE. She could picture them, bronze and scarlet against the snow, light-years from home. But that wasn't the surprise: "Not in this town. These highways always go commercial. We'll be lucky to get our money out." His cadence struck Hazel, as if Jerry had traveled light-years and come back to himself again.

"Mistakes are unavoidable in any creative venture," he reminded her as they left the car. "They plague all invention, all discovery. Columbus lost on the ocean. The current turmoil at the plant. A trans-Canada pipeline ahead of its time. We have to come up with a better idea. Maybe a power transformer on the river. It'll take time, public hearings, dynamite. But they'll buy it. The plant put this burg on the map." Hazel could see it, a dark blot against the faint feathery swirls of mountain ranges. Jerry took her arm and they walked over and around the clutter of construction materials, toward the house. The lone blue tower loomed like an enormous bruise and Hazel averted her gaze. For shame, to spare the house embarrassment in its denuded state, its being ravaged, an abducted woman forced to play the harlot.

They crossed over into the dark, Jerry's eyes catching a glint off the new stainless-steel trim before he switched on the light.

He searched her face briefly, then peered into a folder, while Hazel repeated what she'd prepared beforehand, a litany of praise. Until, losing steam, she became silent and walked to the picture window at the dining end of the elongated kitchen, down two steps to look out toward the foothills. The view had consoled her so many times. Framing her eyes with her hands cupped against the glass, she looked into the dark. A dark as opaque as if the window had been covered with black paint. She stared on until a shape drew out of the night and became recognizable as the form of a tree against the very edge of the glass. Hazel gazed up the grooved channels of the dark column to the crotch where it branched into the vase formation of the elm.

"Jerry," she said, "the tree." She felt suffocated, as if she was being crowded by something large and indomitable. Jerry's back was to her, head down. "Come look at this, Hazel, if you want something to celebrate."

She walked over and switched off the overhead light. It was dark in the room, and gradually the elm showed plainly, in relief at the window, backed by the lighter sky, dead center, with the aspect of suppliant, its leaves in its hands.

"For God's sake, Hazel." He was lowering at her through the gloom, then shook it off and sighed. "I admit, the tree will have to go. It's unfortunate. But don't forget, somebody's getting one hell of a bundle of cordwood."

He turned on the light and opened the new refrigerator, taking a bottle of champagne from its brilliant interior. "I didn't want to have to tell you like this." His smile was tentative. "But we're being transferred. To Cleveland. They have an energy project in mind for the whole region. Put Lake Erie to work. It'll be a step up for us," and he began to depict their future to Hazel, bringing down from the factory-fresh laminate cupboards two goblets that had survived from a wedding present of twelve.

They'd had suburban life, village life. Now it would be Hazel in the big city, Hazel at the center of modern life, furthering urban renewal, school busing, and consumer action. They'd splurge on a hot new car—leave the sissy jobs for the Japanese. There was still hope for the world, even those old dead lakes resurrected and brought into harness. Under the overhead fluorescent light with its relentless circuit of electrons battering tungsten, Jerry's eyes sunk in his head like knotholes. The dark figure at the window was eclipsed by Hazel's mirrored image, where she saw herself standing as dumb as a post. Yet the tree loomed with an actual unflinching presence, more insistent than any past she could recall or any future she might conceive.

Ghost Dance

FIRST THING when we reached each other, coming from opposite directions across the open field, the woman startled me,
throwing both arms around me in a big hug. "I was hoping I'd
meet Susan's sister—even if it took a fire." She was strong and
by then I was already overcome, coughing and drawing back
with a helpless smile, pointing at the fire with tears streaming
from my eyes. Susan was back at the house, calling the fire
department, and had sent me ahead to assess the blaze, as though
my opinion might help, as though as a last resort I might fling
myself upon the flames. I'd been on the verge of reminding her
of a hedge fire when we were children, how when sent for water
she'd struggled back with a glassful. But Susan was in no laughing mood, yanking out her bottom lip in a repetitive anxious
habit I'd told her for years made her resemble the village idiot.
Her freckles ran in a tarnished wash over her thin redhead's
skin, sickly with fear. I couldn't really blame her. It was her
infant daughter who had been sleeping one afternoon and then
was dead in her crib. Since then, a moment's peace had never
been any longer.

I'd set out on my mission with confidence, the fire in the

distance certainly no real danger, no cause for all the fuss. Some dry grass sizzling in the noonday sun, roiling smoke. Besides, I liked the smell. But when I'd passed beyond her rail fence and the breeze, suddenly perceptible, prickled the hair on my neck, I could see that if the fire ever once got going, there'd be nothing to break its sweep over the acres of dryland. How quickly it could devour Susan's wooden fences, the corral and barns, even the house, and the sheep grazing down by the road, panicked, might follow each other into the flames. By the time I'd met up with the woman who approached me from the only other house visible from Susan's property, I was feeling my just portion of alarm.

"You think it'll be all right?" I managed finally, supposing she was their neighbor, Mrs. Carroll, whom Susan said everyone called Carroll. She'd said I'd know why when I saw her and she did look tough—in a sexy, cowgirl fashion, all duded up. I held my face away, wiping off the last tears with my sleeve.

"I reckon." She shrugged, indifferent, as though she was passing overhead in the silver jet sparking the blue. When she'd hugged me, her platinum curls rasped like a tumbleweed, unaffected by the breeze. Amid the seamed landscape of her powdered and rouged cheeks, her eyes flashed blue and shallow as arroyos. I felt diminished, standing beside her, as though she were the West incarnate, enduring drought, Indian wars, cloudbursts, and dust devils. And I felt lost in the immense dusty land that extended far away to the mountains, except where the narrow valley coiled green along the irrigation.

"I'm fifty-three," she offered when our eyes met, not missing a trick. I wasn't that much younger myself. "Still young enough"—her smile a trifle bitter, smacking her narrow flank as though it begot all that savvy, then turning on a real smile to include Susan, who came hurrying from the house, twisting her hands in her long dark skirt. Probably Susan had told her I was newly divorced, the family renegade. She'd told me a few things about Carroll, although she hadn't mentioned how friendly she was, probably didn't like it.

"I'm still shaking," Susan gasped while Carroll gave her a squeeze.

"Your sister's so cute. We were just getting acquainted." Young enough for what, I was mulling it over. Even the mountains wear down to the sea.

"Ever since I saw the smoke I've been running in circles. I've heard how fast it can travel. Feel the wind and the heat. The house." Susan shivered, wiggling her blurred rabbity eyes. I've always considered redheads prone to that comparison, everything about them pink and nervy. "Your house too," she assured Carroll.

Carroll shrugged toward the small dark man who appeared out of the smoke and delivered a diminutive bow in our direction before he went on, slapping laconically at licks of flame, using a damp gunny sack. He crossed a shallow ravine which dipped through the mesquite. "He started it," Carroll asserted loudly, and the man stopped, motioning, hands opened in appeal. He began to mumble in Spanish, waving the sack more energetically for emphasis, before he vanished into the smoke again. Carroll commented that it was a fool thing to do, burning when there was a wind. She figured he'd luck out, though; probably nothing much would suffer. With her fuchsia nail job and sausage curls, she was a painted Ma Barker. She and Susan eyed each other and then the hombre; out of patience with incompetence, with Mexicans, it seemed to me.

"*Vaya, vaya.*" Carroll clapped her hands as he reappeared. As if she was saying "Scat!" Let him risk his own house and family, not hers. His culpability was as much in the cards as range wars and heatstroke. Over the brim of his visor cap, *John Deere* was stitched in yellow script.

"I hope he'll be okay," I said when he'd gone into the smoke again. Both women stared at me, Carroll with the steadiness of

a gunfighter, Susan with her frosted irony. "I mean," I pushed
on, just as stubborn, "when he's in there a long time with all
that smoke, I worry that maybe something's happened to him
and he won't come back out." I *was* worried and thought they
should be too. Mexican or not, he was after all a man risking
danger with every foray into the fire. They'd been spoiled by too
many housemaids from over the border, content to order them
about in gutter Spanish. A dollar exchanged for thousands of
pesos. The man flailing the open spaces seemed as devalued.

Eyes level on the flames, Carroll said, "It's his doing."

"I don't think he should have to die for it." After a pause, she
laughed, tossing her head, the stagnant curls jogging a beat. She
hugged me again. "No, I don't expect he should." She winked
at Susan. "Your sister's cute. A right cute Yankee."

A hollow victory: greenhorn, bearer of New England rectitude
faint upon the prickly pear. Fuck it. Let them tear down the
Rocky Mountains to run the infernal combustion engine, strip
and flood the red man's sacred places. My poor sad Yankee skin
already felt tender from a few moments in their sun. When my
dejected gaze met Carroll's, she winked again. Like she said, she
was young enough, just dandy. Jeans laced to a fare-thee-well
over a comfortable stomach, leather belt and boots. Susan and
I were thinner, no small achievement in some circles, but out on
the range it seemed a morbid preoccupation.

The fire engine came, bolting along the county road, siren
blasting, swinging into the lane alongside Carroll's land, brushing down the alfalfa and grasses in swaths. Several men dropped
off as it slowed, rushing toward the fire, shouldering tanks of
extinguisher, fitting gas masks. John Deere would surprise them,
materializing in their midst like a genie out of a bottle. The
danger seemed slight, now that help had arrived, and I said that
about John Deere. Carroll laughed, but Susan stood still, with
her hair blown over her face. She could never keep a barrette
there, always the child with her hair in her face, and I moved

to stand close to her, reaching out to fix it. Without opening her eyes she snapped, "I'm praying."

Carroll volunteered, "I was watching it more than an hour before I came out—when I saw you coming. I was going to call the department, but Tufts said, 'Leave it be. Ain't none of our affair.' " Susan's eyes flew open at that, and when the Mexican came in view she turned her back, muttering that she was walking over to the truck. It was obvious she didn't want company. As if in answer to prayer, the wind had shifted, bending the blaze back upon itself. "I guess we weren't serious enough," I apologized for Susan.

"Tufts wouldn't turn around and see for himself. Not him. After that I didn't say one word. If he don't care about the house or nothin', let him burn up in there. I know him, he's not turned around yet. Television yapping in the corner." She kicked, as though at something yapping, her grim observation deposited on her lips like a sediment. "Our twentieth the end of the month. Feels like life."

It figured, Tufts could only be her husband. I remembered hearing that he'd lost both legs somehow and was confined to a wheelchair and she took care of him all alone. Across the field, her bleached adobe looked as bleak as a failed marriage.

"I left my husband," I confided with a racing heart, admitting a crime. "Nearly six months ago, but I still can't believe it. I keep thinking I'll wake up." The fire was dying back fast and John Deere headed in the same direction as Susan, bearding the lion in her den. A couple of firemen straggled that way too; the smoke thinned and the chemical foam melted in a sludge. "I'm sorry," I added, meaning her husband, my husband, divorce.

Her face warned—don't be sorry for me. "I thought there was something about you," she said, examining her cuticle as though probing for precise sensitivity. "I reckon you might . . . if there's another man."

"*You* might" curled up the end of my tongue. I could imagine she'd loved different men. Her bosom was commodious and there was that look in her eye that meant business. "It wasn't that. I just couldn't stay." It seemed too complicated to explain.

"You might stay, if you hated him the way I hate Tufts. Can't stop chewing on it." Her jaw crunched off sideways.

I was sorry I'd begun, spreading divorce like an Eastern contagion. Then when you had it, what did you have but something mean and ruined. "I stayed married for eighteen years. We saw a marriage counselor for three. She was disheartened and so were we. Nothing got any better, if not much worse." The cottonwood tree in the middle of the field became visible again, wreathed in tatters of lifting smoke, each of its leaves ignited singly, as though it were decorated with myriad candles. Susan came strolling back from the fire engine, the worry and irritation on her face replaced by the more familiar distraction and sadness. John Deere, by the truck, stood with bowed head, awaiting deportation. Susan said the chief was packing up, everybody could leave. "Too bad about the tree." In the early days, she'd told me, the cottonwood would have been a hanging tree, not many so wide and spreading. Mostly it had been the young ones who got the rope, fifteen-, sixteen-year-old rustlers, feckless enough to get caught.

"Don't you worry." Carroll patted Susan's arm. "It'll come right back, for sure. I've seen them black as char, stripped as if locusts had passed. For them a fire's not a whole lot hotter than most days in this hellhole." The remaining smoke dilated the flaming leaves in a pulsing rhythm like black light. "Anniversary cake." She elbowed me. Her mood recalled an old grade-school burlesque, sung at the top of our lungs: "Oh, how we danced on the night we were wed/If you think we danced then, you're cracked in the head."

Susan said the man who'd started the fire was Mr. Lamas, their next neighbor to the north. He'd been ill and had fallen behind. When he'd started burning it hadn't seemed that windy.

He'd apologized to Susan again and again, for alarming her, and Susan said she guessed she'd forgive him—for my sake. In her opinion I was sanctimonious, although she sounded the same to me when she went on to suggest his illness had more to do with the bottle than with a thermometer.

"Everybody I know's got a bottle problem, 'cept you and the doctor." Susan's husband was a botanist, but in that rural region he was affectionately the doctor.

"Right?" Carroll included me in world-weariness. Susan and Jim kept liquor in the house and offered it to guests, but they didn't touch it—maybe a sip with company to be polite. In the ten years since their little girl had died they'd gone on, worked hard, and started a second family. But the last thing they wanted was a good time or even a breathing spell. When as a child Susan had a low-grade chronic bronchitis, I'd envied her, thinking she got more of our mother's attention. But this last misfortune had been too much, and both Susan and Jim had a look about them, almost daft, as though, set to a task and warned of its absolute imperative, they had yet to be told exactly what to do and when it would be finished.

"Now, Tufts. That's a bottle problem." Carroll slid her sly smile my way when Susan didn't react. "The doctor knows. Tufts got sugar, but he wouldn't listen to anybody. He knew better. They had to take both legs, one at a time. Propped him in that chair. He just sets the bottles on the floor when he don't toss one through the window. When he wants something off me, he knocks that stick on the floor. Like he's calling a dog. One of these days," she said pleasantly, "I'll ram it down his throat." She drew cigarettes from her pocket, offering me one, and I took it. "Your sister's a live one," she tried teasing Susan, who scarcely nodded. We lit up in silence, letting the smoke calm us a little.

"I quit years ago," I said. "But I'm going like a chimney since the breakup. For a while I didn't give a damn what they did to me and now I'm stuck with them." Susan fidgeted, glaring indeterminately. She didn't approve of tough talk or smoking, or standing around, none of it being what she would have judged productive, what she thought life must be about—at least in the absence of clearer indications. I thought of her dragging the irrigation hoses around the fields all summer, rationing water, moving the sheep to greener pastures. Her friends, other well-to-do women, worked as frenetically, mowing acres of hay, digging leach fields, digging their own graves. Their ironing and dishes were left for the maids.

Reflectively, Carroll removed a trace of tobacco from her lip, holding her cigarette with the flair of ornamentation. "Tufts is my second. My first died of a heart attack, left me my daughter and a load of bills. Tufts comes along and helps me out. We built this place from nothing, made the horses pay. There were good years. Guess there always are." Behind her, Susan slit her throat with her finger. She'd mentioned Carroll to me, liked her well enough, felt sorry for her, although she considered her common, making a mess of everything and spreading the news. Susan had always been bored and humiliated by complaint, and when Carroll said, "My daughter says I should get the hell out," she winced and said she had to be getting home. I told her to go on, I'd be along soon. Against the sky, in spite of her purposeful stride, Susan made me think of Mr. Lamas, the wanderer on the plains, a speck in time. The last of the firemen had made it to the truck, and they pulled away, giving a blast of the horn as they passed the Carroll home. Probably Susan thought I was common too in my new outlaw status. She'd never criticized me for leaving my marriage, but to her it was an unimaginable rupture, as though you had taken a daughter out and left her in a tree.

"They'd hire me down to Durango," Carroll continued when we were alone, that old salt of endurance and forlorn hopes. "My daughter cooks on one of them big ranch concerns. They can always use extra hands in the kitchen." The thought of her peeling spuds and flipping griddle cakes at her age made me want to use my remaining strength to dig a hole for both of us. Off across the burnt grass in the shimmering heat, I thought I could make out a deep green river, feel it pull toward infinity.

"Probably they'd let me work with the horses too. Four or five of mine are down there. He says all I've ever done is sit on my backside. Driving that tractor all over creation, breaking horses, some of them wild mustangs. He's the one sold them off. Next time he pokes me in the ass with that stick—pardon my French." I didn't mind and Susan was gone.

I knelt down to grind out my cigarette, pocketing the butt, rueful and self-conscious about my ways in front of Dale Evans. Waste not, want not—environmentally a royal pain. Maybe her tale of woe was no different from any other Western yarn, meant to separate the men from the boys. Days passed and she and Tufts didn't find a word to say. At night she locked her bedroom door. With the sun directly overhead, before us the slurry of foamy black grass, the smoldering tree rose like a scaffold from the days when people took the law into their own hands.

"All of them think it's the money. In a way it is, maybe. After I've put in so much. My life's here. I want to hang on long as I can. Don't want to let him beat me. I've threatened to get a lawyer, but he says he's not signing nothing. I hate to give money to lawyers when there's not much left anyways."

Just as I was nodding my head, the retort of a gunshot made both of us jump and scatter a little, as though we were in cahoots and deserved to be killed on the spot. Carroll quieted first, pale and then bright red, while I couldn't stop shaking. Shots kept blasting away as she was calmly helping herself to another cigarette, tapping it first on her watch. "Lunchtime, I reckon," she said when it was still. "Well, he can hold his horses till I'm done visiting. I'm sorry, hon." There was a bracket of bloodless tooth marks above her lips.

"He wheels himself into the back storeroom, aims out the window. Out at the old bunkhouse. Won't nobody get in the line of fire—he's chased everybody off. Leaves it propped beside him, up against the chair. Gets on your nerves. I've told him, 'Go on and shoot. Get it over with.' " She stood ramrod stiff, as though facing a firing squad.

"I don't think you should have to die for it," I mumbled, on shaky ground. But she remembered Mr. Lamas and smiled. "Sometimes it seems easier."

There were mountains in all directions, miles beyond the wide valley floor. To the east, the Absarokas swayed in the heat like ghost tepees, luminous in folds of pastel sandstone, vigilant evocations of what had been. Susan had told me that Carroll had a reputation in the valley. The ditch rider, for one, had talked about her, one morning when Susan had watched for him in the fields at six-thirty, to ask about increasing their water delivery. While they waited for the water to head, they could see Carroll, way across the intervening land, working a palomino filly before the heat of the day, both of them trailing pale hair against the purple mountains. He said it was the customary opinion of folks around there that they deserved one another, she and Tufts. Carroll had a reputation with horses too and Susan said it was spellbinding to watch her. Even at that distance you could sense the concentration, each responding to the other, linked by the lead. Almost as if they were dancing. Susan had glanced up at the ditch rider, a good-looking young man with a cigarette untended in his hand. He grinned and flicked the ash when he caught Susan's glance, shook his head. "Just thinking," he murmured. For some reason, Susan said, she blushed.

"He won't let me touch a thing. Lets the bills go. You'd think one day I'd smarten up." Carroll was turning the diamond on her finger, big as a rock. "Maybe I'll sell it"—she caught me looking. I held up my own bare hand. Maybe the ditch rider had it right and nothing should be done.

Her house, beyond the field, through the blaze of mesquite, appeared insubstantial, as though it might vanish when you turned your back. It didn't look run-down so much as desolate, shutters fastened all around, the yard raked, dust caked on leathery shrubs and thorns, the loneliness of extremity. Susan's children were afraid to trespass there, with Tufts yelling at them and setting the dog loose. They'd heard the shooting too and made up stories about a haunted house and murder, as if they knew.

"The Christians have been putting in their hand. Stop for me Sundays and for prayer meeting. Tufts thinks that's rich, like I wouldn't know better and might smoke a cigarette in the pew. But they've been real nice. A lot have offered me a place to stay if I need it." She pulled her mouth sideways—she needed it.

"You'll try anything sometimes. I had my palm read once. Amounts to the same thing: everything will be roses in the sweet by-and-by. The church of the wishful thinkers." I slowed down, too easy an irony as good as a death blow. Carroll listened intently, her weight thrown back, one foot tapping. As though she were teaching a trick horse to count, as though I might do the incredible and sum everything up.

"I've been poor," I admitted, "or what feels like poor to me. Doing without a car, paying doctors' bills on what I make as a secretary. I've walked miles and miles carrying a suitcase over hill and dale. Like a Bible salesman. When I ride the buses, I see the old women close up. The ones who don't have anybody. The way they hobble on the steps, tiny baby steps in black tie shoes. The drivers wouldn't dream of giving them a break, waiting for them to find seats. Old ladies rolling and pitching, fumbling in their pocketbooks, as though a token would get them out of jail." I turned away, stamping my foot. "Goddamn," I said, as though I could always be angry and never sad.

Carroll slipped an arm around my shoulder. "You're all right—you just got some smoke in your eyes. It's time I get on home. Before he gives another holler. You and Susan come get some cherries; they're ready now. Some for the doctor. When Tufts fell out of his chair, Jim came right over, called back to ask how he was. After he'd nearly broke his neck too, stumbling over the bottles. It was a terrible thing, what happened to their little girl. Makes you feel tenderhearted even when Susan is snippety."

I'd been feeling snippety myself, until she said that, wondering what a botanist had ever done to get so much extra attention, wondering why she didn't wheel Tufts out into the desert and leave him there. I watched while she moved away, deliberately, like one condemned, toward where Tufts was waiting and waiting. Feeling guilty as if I should have gone with her, imagined trying to get a bite down at gunpoint. When Carroll was approaching her long, whitewashed fence, the pooled dust glittering everywhere in a mica powder that hurt my eyes, I lowered my head and turned toward Susan's, the sun brimming from behind with the aura of a sombrero.

This time the roar of the gunshot ran through me as if I'd been bushwhacked, only I didn't fear for myself, whirling around to look back, grateful beyond belief that it was Carroll standing in the middle of the side corral, holding a rifle and firing up in the air. She wasn't in any hurry, gravely emptying the gun, the shots coming at distinct and measured intervals until the final retort faded away. Then she crossed over to the barn and went inside, coming back out empty-handed and padlocking the door before she went into the house.

Although she hadn't nodded or waved, there was something personal in the stern discharge of the gun, like a salute. Or I took it that way. I turned toward the Absarokas, my feet seeming to lift of their own accord, linked to formal indigenous rhythms that footsteps had pounded into the earth for all time, exhausting themselves in a last effort to make medicine roll down like water, going down to defeat. The glowing peaks appeared to billow and shift in their enduring folds, shadowing the old ghost dance of the plains in haunting supplication, for what had been and would never come again.

Elderberries and Souls

UNDER THE ELMS that would last forever, as fixed in their roots as stars in patterns, Joey and I would walk in the summer dark along the river and take the night's last ferry to Ohio and back. It was a favor to me, Joey only anxious to make the return from Ohio, to get to the white filigree love seat that Ruby had placed near the bank for river watching; he didn't know why we had to make the crossing at all. Neither did I, but I had to be out on the river. It was part of what would happen next, and there were other reasons too I couldn't say: the dark land stretched on the far side, our progression stately as a pavane upon the deep. Often at that hour, no cars were waiting at the slip and we, the only travelers, walked rapidly up the gangplank with a nod to the kid who threw the rope, and were momentarily on our way, amid the clatter and scrape on the dock, the surging engine's reverse. Then we'd be making the run on the water, mounted on its back with the current underneath like Behemoth. The air streaming down the mountain pass taking my hair, the ferry lights quick rocket bursts in the foam—I gave myself to it. While Joey, hung out over the railing, glanced back repeatedly with his perplexed overfond regard; wondering about me the way he always did,

along for the ride, eager to touch Ohio like base and head back
to home shore. I became lost in the dark, feeling the water move,
impartial, cadenced, right then not thinking of Joey at all. Uncle
Kurt, I'd be longing inside myself. He wasn't my flesh-and-blood
uncle but my stepmother's brother. After she married my father
and came to live with us, she was always telling stories about
her life and people, exhibiting their facets and fires, jewels of
adornment which I felt privileged to admire, made to desire.

"My brother Kurt," she would begin, praising him with might
and main. "He was always a beautiful boy and then he grew so
tall." I imagined his austere brow elevated until it brushed among
the elm boughs. "You can't imagine how intelligent he was. How
sensitive. And later so passionate. Although he never was one to
run after the girls. He's different, you know." She'd nod in her
knowing way, and I'd know she was referring to the difference
that was like looking deep into things, clear through to souls
that ran in the dark underneath all the rest of a person and
carried them on to their long home. No matter to us that Kurt
was her brother, my uncle, and married. We sang his legend
over the mending and potato peelings, intimate as conspirators.
"He thinks you're special, Silvy," she confided. "Like a queen."

Joey didn't think I was a queen, but he did think I was different
from the other girls in town, probably because I didn't come
from there, didn't know anything about football, and didn't care.
And because of the late-night boat rides. We dated whenever I
was staying in town with my step-grandparents, Ruby and Terrence, who owned and operated a small inn and restaurant, set
right on the banks of the Ohio River. That summer, when I was
sixteen, I worked for them the whole season as the hired girl,
hanging out baskets of coarse muslin sheets, running errands on
foot to Main Street, and operating the mangle in the back kitchen,
which had been a servant's bedroom when the hotel was a riv-
erfront mansion built for some coal baron. Ruby and I got along
from the very first, when she and I became related. "With you

and me it was love at first sight," she declared, giving me extra money for ice cream at the dairy store.

In the middle of August, Uncle Kurt was coming to stay for a few days, to visit his family while his wife went to Salt Lake City. I was waiting for him, still going out with Joey, to the picture show or sandlot games to watch him pitch, trying for experience, tasting his hot sweet kisses when we returned from the ferry trips. But putting him off about taking his mother's car out to the highway, then down along to the old rotted wharf to park. Joey didn't push too hard, although each vacation he had more in mind for us to do together, put his hands more urgently around my waist, lifted me closer. Once he whispered, "Angel," against my hair. It bewitched me like an inscription on a tombstone. It made me uneasy. For I didn't know what he really wanted, what was supposed to happen next. As long as Joey was coming by to date me, dependable as the ferry boat traversing the river, giving me bits of experience, my thoughts and dreams were all of Uncle Kurt. My body seemed scarcely to exist.

"Silvy," someone would call sometime each day, "Joey's on the phone." I'd answer, my insides a quick fist, that clench, distant and in the dark, the nearest thing to passion I'd ever felt with Joey. I ignored it, though I never thought to refuse his summons.

The night before Uncle Kurt was arriving, I was waiting for Joey out on the porch with Ruby, who spent her evening time, after her work was finished, sitting there to watch the river, the darkness draining down on the polished water, around her the hanging swing, the glider and iron chairs piled with bleached cushions, velvet petunias flourishing in boxes like muted horns.

"It's grand here on the river, Silvy," Ruby said, to begin another evening, her voice dreamy in the drawing dusk. "I'll never understand your folks, moving away from the river. Their view's a sight, I know, but it doesn't compare. And this breeze."

She smiled around her, pushing the glider with one foot, her swollen leg resting on a propped cushion. In the close summer night, with the ferry haunting the river below, going silently back and forth like Ruby's glider, the awnings striped over the porch, the iron railings twisting, flowers shining, I was waiting for Joey. But while Ruby talked about the river, old times and the family, his arrival seemed an intrusion, nothing I'd ever wanted.

"Kurt just idolized Claudia from the day he saw her," Ruby said. "That was when she was sixteen, and that same day he said, 'I'm going to marry that girl.' He did too. My, but she was pretty as a picture." That picture of Claudia was on Ruby's piano, across from the one of Uncle Kurt when he was in the army, their smiles tilted toward each other, as if that first meeting was preserved forever. Claudia's teeth gleamed, reflecting the glisten of pearls around her neck, and somewhere, not showing, was the deep part Uncle Kurt knew about, the part that mattered. My own high-school picture was there too, proof that some pictures were not pretty. I'd moved it back beside the one of Terrence in the buggy he bought new when he and Ruby were courting. It seemed to fit that setting, my sturdy neck, hair scalped into braids, beside the bygone country scene. It showed plainly in the picture that I didn't belong to the Pringles, not really, my face and hair all wrong.

"Now that Kurt's beginning his practice, they'll likely be starting their family. It's been eight years." Ruby's voice sounded wistful and I thought maybe she was wishing for some real grandchildren—the blood kind, the look-alike kind. But she added, "Sometimes a baby helps folks get along."

It shocked me, the thought of Uncle Kurt needing help, needing anything. Perhaps something I could give him, up in the front room on the third floor, up in the dust that lay in twilight, coated the narrow stairway winding on up to the widow's walk, the windows low on the painted floor, wavy panes of river light

shadowing the water-stained wallpaper, elm branches and wind
rattling the roof. My face fired in the evening breeze as if held
to a burning glass.

"There's a barge coming, Silvy. Moving coal to Pittsburgh, I
reckon." Ruby thought I'd be impressed by big river traffic, like
a nine-year-old, like she was. "Maine—Augusta on the Kenne-
bec, New Hampshire—Concord on the Merrimack, Vermont—
Montpelier on the Winooski," she hummed to herself, making
her check of the old information, held for sixty-some years behind the pale flowery blue of her eyes. "Ohio," she told me, not
for the first time, "that's Indian for beautiful river. This must
have been a beautiful river for a long time. Kurt will be here in
the morning." She nodded, as if announcing another barge. Not
that I had to be told, counting off the days on the Pringle Funeral
Home calendar, which hung by the kitchen sink. Half the busi-
nesses in town were Pringle.

Then Joey was coming toward us, up the stairs out of the
clicking dark of summer insects, clumsy and restrained by his
football shamble, which was developed for major defense, not
for simply coming round to take a girl to the Saturday picture
show. Away from her family, from Ruby, who glowed creamy
pale and soft as a cotton boll in her summer dress, its front
polka-dotted with flour spots to absorb the grease spatters from
cooking, her fleshy arms thick tallow props for her bosom, which
only drastic corseting could subdue. Away from Ruby and her
nightly serenade to the beautiful Ohio.

"Evening, Mrs. Pringle." Joey nodded, looking quickly at me.
"Hot enough for you?"—smiling at me.

"Glory. I'd say so," Ruby answered, meaning everything was
grand. "Might rain tonight."

"Garden needs it. Well, lady"—Joey winked at Ruby, talking
to me—"let's get walkin' if we're going to see the picture show
and get you back for your boat ride. Your granddaughter sure
thinks a heap of that ferry." His voice broke, slightly hoarse,

but he rolled his eyes, grinning, all of it part of his appreciation. The gold bridgework, laid in where a bygone tackle had plundered his jaw, flashed. He looked proud of his war wounds, proud to escort a girl with mysterious intentions when another would have been content to go to the Wagonwheel for a milk shake. His pleasure gave me the fidgets and I didn't smile. Not that Joey was discouraged. He took my arm as we started up Main Street, as if he had in his possession a rare and obscure manuscript which only a lifetime of devotion could decipher.

"If it's not my girl from the North," Uncle Kurt was saying in the morning, holding me strong against his chest, his head off somewhere above where a six-foot-three head is, and I was smelling his cotton shirt, smoke and starch, and his soul, as if that too were a thing to be smelled. Then he lifted Ruby off her feet while I stood by, overheated and crushed, resembling something run through the mangle.

"My girl from the North." The North stretched away, up and over us with the house, on toward the third floor, where Uncle Kurt was needing me. When the phone rang I knew, restoring myself with deep breaths on the way to answer it, knew it would be Joey, pushing his way in.

"I got the afternoon off. We'll take the canoe. Okay? And swim, like I said?" His insipid drawl dragged on me like reins and made him sound halfhearted too. Go yourself, I wanted to interrupt, but I was saying yes, just like I had to go.

Out on the river in the raving heat of mid-afternoon, we trailed our way downstream in the yellow canvas canoe. It seemed preposterous that it had been my idea in the first place. From the bow, I glanced back at Joey, who was already glazed with sweat. It stiffened his hair where it rose up in a pompadour, and clung to his forehead. Salty and repulsive, if I licked him. I was perverse and couldn't help thinking about that while we dipped our paddles into the river, a victim of the heat fallen impassive beneath us.

"Silvy," Joey said when I'd turned away. "Let's go up one of the coves where there's a swimming hole."

"That's why I wore my suit, you know." I shook the man's shirt I wore hard at him, my back still turned. He'd already heard me agree on the phone, although it was true I wasn't interested now, wanted to be back at the hotel, printing the daily specials on the dining-room chalkboard, making it as neat as possible.

"Don't you want to?" he persisted, the vibration in his voice a warning, as if he might be getting angry.

"Sure," I said. When I glanced back I could see his mood changing, his eyes narrow, the muscle along his jaw ticking in a deliberate beat. If I wasn't careful, he'd have me plunked back at the hotel, wondering how I was going to get him to call me again, for when Joey was aroused and smoldering, he interested and troubled me—until he was coming around reliably again.

I decided to start a conversation. Usually it was pretty one-sided, with me rattling on about a subject as long as I wanted; anything would do, for I could always get his attention. When I questioned Joey, he just grinned or joked around, though I would make a good listener if he'd give me a chance.

"I don't know how you guys can practice in this heat. I'd think you'd have heart attacks or strokes." I did think so, passing the school on my way to the swimming pool, seeing the boys on the football field, unrecognizable in pads and helmets, plowing into each other, counting out interminable jumping jacks and push-ups.

"You hot?" He flicked a spray of tepid water in my face when I turned around, grinning at me. "You get used to it. Besides, I need the scholarship." His shrug reminded me that everything was set. After high school he was going to the state university to major in business administration—how much could you say about that? He stared off toward the bend, his gaze as drab as his future.

I hurried to fill up the silence, and he was grinning again when

I said, "Probably I won't go to school. Certainly not right away. I want to travel, see a lot of different places. Live in New York City. Maybe I'll be an artist's model and you can see me in the art museums," a notion that had him fanning himself to beat the band, gasping for water like a dying man. When Joey listened to me, seeming so amused and interested, I wanted to go on and tell him more, things I was serious about.

"What I'd really like is to live by myself, alone somewhere. On a farm with animals and a garden. I'd sleep up high in a loft, maybe in a log cabin, and right under a window. Smell pine trees and listen to the wind, watch the stars all night long. Not have things either. Like appliances or furnaces. No electricity at all."

"Silvy, you'll freeze your ass." But he was with me, thinking about it along with me, as if maybe he could be there too, working a plow or splitting wood. I was having an inner vision of my life in that place of long winters, drifting snows, windows frozen from an Arctic cold that chimed from the spheres, forests resting in their ancient state while somewhere Uncle Kurt, dark-browed amid the blowing snow, was seeking me, always just on the point of arriving.

"You'd need somebody to take care of you. Somebody big and strong." Joey was ready to take the part, and I remembered he was only one step from a hill-farm boy himself, in spite of his college ambitions. Ruby had told me that his father had come down from the mountains when he was fifteen, boarding with a family in exchange for chores and going to high school, finally bettering himself until he was a vice president at one of the local banks. Probably Joey could as easily work himself back in the opposite direction. But I couldn't imagine my dream with Joey. "I'm just blabbing," I muttered. "Probably I'll end up like everybody else. Going to school." I didn't add, "Getting married and having babies."

The last of the town was passing by, windows showery with

light, everything hushed and lonesome while beyond the ferry shimmered, like something shaken by the heat. Once the *Delta Queen* had docked in town and Joey came unexpectedly to give me a tour. We watched people eating in the circular dining room, the surrounding luster of buffed mahogany showing them at their best, and one of the berths was open so we could see in and imagine spending the night. It was an actual riverboat, one that could take us clear to New Orleans. "I know you're partial to travel by steamer," Joey teased, and I knew he was thinking of a time we might take a trip together. It extinguished my excitement, although the calliope sounding all over town had brought nearly everyone to come on board. New Orleans had to be more than someplace you could get to capably and by excursion. It had to spring upon you in the night.

The hotel was far behind now. Ruby and Uncle Kurt would be together in the kitchen, Ruby at the mangle finishing up the sheets, Uncle Kurt smoking, his face amused and gratified as they talked. Always with his mother, there was that other expression too, of nearly unbearable tenderness, as though he was watching her growing old.

Joey and I paddled in close to shore, into the tangle of alder, locust, and willow, the water's surface layered with floating debris at the shore. A condom washed in the yellow leaves, limp and incriminating exposed that way. I leaned toward Ohio, hoping Joey didn't see it, or at least that he wouldn't say anything. Nearby a drowned log brought in tow a scum of sudsy bubbles. "What's that, Joey?" I pointed. "The brownish foam."

"I couldn't tell you that, Silvy. You'd be too shocked." I knew then he'd seen it, making a mystery of frogs' eggs, him and his one-track mind. Thinking things and wanting me to think them too. "You wouldn't swim if I told you. You'd be all discombobulated." He enjoyed saying that, both of us on the honor roll at school. As if I'd be impressed. But I could let it pass, because we were turning into the cove and I wondered how it would be in the woods away from open water. I let him go on looking secretive and protective, the last word on animal reproduction.

The entrance to the tributary was concealed, so it seemed Joey headed us straight into the bank. We ducked to cover our faces in our arms, itching all over with the plague of excited mosquitoes, the drag of breaking webs. It was suddenly tropical, the creek sluggish, twisting narrowly, ferns solemn and outsized, as though they might grow into the trees of a primeval rain forest. An alligator might slither from the bank. But then as abruptly we emerged into a high arched grove of hickory, oak, beech, and sycamore, the low ferns dense in their scent of earth and spore, with the sky laced green, the stream running green. My pale skin emitted a phosphorescent glow, as if green were the color of darkness.

"There's the pool." Joey's voice glanced, high-pitched with excitement, as he pointed ahead. "Beyond that giant rock." Rock layers loomed out of the forest floor, rising far over our heads, the water deepening as we came into the basin and glided over to the side to tie up to a slender branch. The old trees pressed down. Ferns, burdened with beaded spore, reflected in the water. When Joey reached for my hand to pull me out of the canoe, his was warm and embracing, as though it could have held all of me.

I stepped away from him on the bank. "Last one in's a rotten egg," I croaked in a tone I'd meant to sound lofty. Joey stepped between me and the water, reaching out to open the buttons of my father's white shirt, the shirt loosening and unraveling between his fingers like a gauze dressing. It was like a trance, watching as it fell away, revealing the half-moons of my breasts swelling out of the black bathing suit. His eyes, when I looked up to meet them, had gone plaintive as birdsong in the woods as his fingers reached lower and took hold of the fastening to my shorts, his movement abruptly more urgent. We both heard the pop as the button gave way.

"I can do it myself," I snapped, yanking away, and in one fluid motion I stepped out of my shorts and dove shallowly into the pool, swimming down the cone of rock as though into a volcano. When I surfaced, Joey was off behind me, lying face downward beside the water, regarding me with his serious look, not the angry one but like it. He was still dressed, just his feet bare, sticking out like growths on the forest floor. I stretched out on the water and shut my eyes. When I turned my head to look at him again, he was facing the other way, but he spoke. "Silvy, you're a goddamn tease."

I pulled out of the water and went to sit in the canoe, avoiding his eyes when he got up and came to take his place at the other end, his head rigid, as though he bore it on a platter.

All the time we drifted down the channel and out onto the river into the waiting heat, I kept myself stiff and arched away from him too. We didn't have anything left to say, working hard against the current, taking the heat, both of us steamed and still furious when at the hotel he held steady while I climbed ashore. Neither of us said goodbye. He bolted into the river without a backward glance. Good riddance. I was unutterably glad to be done with him, hurrying up the wide stone terrace and into the hotel, where I knew Uncle Kurt would be waiting.

Inside the lobby it was peaceful, shady out of the direct sun, with patterns of breezy light flickering in an open fretwork through the slatted shutters onto the walls. The floors dipped, warped and ripply under the thick carpet, its brownish-green color reminiscent of the floods that swept everybody to the second floor once in every decade, as though something actual from the river had been left behind, after the mud was cleared away. The rounded front lobby was outsized, large enough for three plush divans and matching side chairs, the picture-gallery grand piano and two life-sized plaster Mandarins which lifted lampshades high over the varnished mantelpiece toward the ceiling, which would have taken two of Uncle Kurt, end to end, to reach. From the center tin medallion, painted white, hung a crystal chandelier.

Ruby was in the kitchen at the end of the back hall when I came in, kneading bread, beside her in the sink a kettle stuffed with pokeweed, so I knew she'd been down on the riverbank where it grew, dressed as she was in her stockings and garters, the same as for church. I blushed to think maybe she had seen Joey and me, out there in a tizzy. "Ham for supper?" I asked, hoping she hadn't.

"The best you ever had. Off of that piece Clyde brought from over the river." She patted the moldy, leathery rind, which was gritty with brine and saltpeter, smelling of a damp stone cellar. "You and Joey have a good time?" She sounded as though nothing else would have been possible.

"We went up one of the streams, to swim."

"He's a nice boy. I saw in the *Dispatch* he's being scouted for the university. His mother'll be proud."

"Yeah." I picked an apple from the fruit bowl. "Football." I took a big bite.

She arrested her knife partway through a slice of ham and looked up at me, pausing a second before she said, "Maybe he didn't tell you, since you weren't here at the time. Joey's dad took off a few months back. Ran with a woman from the bank, one of the tellers. I hear he's asking Dorey for a divorce, and here he was supposed to be a Catholic. Dorey changed her religion for him, and now she's left with the four boys." Ruby bent down over the ham hock again, sawing away.

I hadn't even known Joey was supposed to be Catholic. I remembered his mother from once when we went inside and she was at the kitchen table. Wearing shorts, she'd seemed about my own age, and I felt shy, especially since the few minutes we were there she never said anything but hello and didn't answer when I said, "Nice to meet you." That had been early in the summer and Ruby said the father had left after Easter. Joey's mother had been hired by the bank where his father had worked. Of course not the same job, and she didn't make much money. The churches in town were helping with the rent until she got on her feet, but it was hard to take charity. Three of the boys worked after school. I changed the conversation back to the ham, and Ruby shifted course without a hitch. Since Joey and I were finished, there wasn't any reason for me to know his life history.

At supper Uncle Kurt sat across from Terrence, his father, who was usually down in the cellar with the sheets and the old Maytag, or into bed early so he could get up in the night for guests or early in the morning for the sheets. I was sitting by the bay window in the evening sun streaming out low from Ohio, the sun just then appearing to halt and hang suspended over the dying day. Ruby was up and down every other second, serving everybody, hardly taking time for a bite herself, until Uncle Kurt put his hand on her arm, telling her to sit—which lasted about five minutes.

Terrence was enjoying his regular mealtime sport, carrying on about modern sinfulness, evolution, government subsidies; blaming socialism on Harry Truman. "If there's a subsidy for empty fields, then I ought to get mine for empty beds." He waggled his finger at Uncle Kurt, who grinned as though this was exactly what he'd come home for. I wondered how it felt to Joey now, whether he hoped his father would never again sit facing him across a table with a meal between them and nothing to say.

Then Uncle Kurt leaned back in his chair, folded his arms across his chest, and directed his piercing gaze across at his father. "You watch. Someday Harry S Truman will be accounted one of the finest Presidents this country has ever had." While Terrence took on about that, stomping on the linoleum, hee-heeing and slapping his knee, Uncle Kurt raised his eyebrows, pliable as birds ruffling themselves, searching into Ruby's eyes and then mine, long and centered as a spell, until I got a hollowed-out, spent feeling. That was the way with Uncle Kurt, to seek out the essence at the heart of things, to speak out boldly.

Ruby was up, bringing us her rhubarb pie with the lattice top, inside cream and butter, the sugared crust shimmering. She stood behind Uncle Kurt, put both hands on his shoulders, saying into his face with a dip of her head, "Silvy's just the same age as Claudia when you brought her home." Uncle Kurt sat tall over the table in his white cotton shirt with the sleeves carefully rolled, smiling at me, while I was thinking he was wise as Solomon, seeing the heart of a woman in a girl, there in the plain, makeshift kitchen, the table up against the refrigerator, in the maize yellow of Ohio sun, the evening light strung out over the river, rhubarb pie luscious in our mouths.

Later, on the porch, whenever the door would open, bringing a shaft of light among us, Uncle Kurt would be looking at me. Then the red point of his cigarette stabbed in the dark again while he and Ruby talked on and I watched the side lights on the ferry jiggle and shake in the water, silvery, so that I imagined they were tambourines and there was music I couldn't hear, waiting for the door to open again to see Uncle Kurt. Across the narrow brick street at the end of the ferry slip, a woman's laugh floated on the air, mysterious, with throaty undertones. A tattoo of heels punctuated her passage up the stairs and into the other hotel, which faced ours from the other side. Ruby and Terrence never talked about that place, as though they hadn't seen it, although it rose brick red against the Southern sky and a blue neon sign read BAR night and day. The ferry slip could have been the river separating them from us. Joey liked to call attention to the people coming and going, and when we walked past he couldn't seem to take his eyes away. He said I wouldn't believe what went on there. "Maybe sometime I'll take you. If you're good," he hinted, only half-joking. When the phone rang in the front lobby, I thought maybe it would be Joey calling, but it was only someone making reservations.

In the morning it was raining. Ruby said Kurt was driving over to Waterville to see his grandmother. "Come with me," he called from the next room, and Ruby urged, "Go." I would be company, since she had to stay by the phone, and bake rolls for the evening meal.

I had to hurry to get ready and she helped me, ironing the blue Swiss-style dress she'd bought and altered for me. She opened my braids and drew some hair into a clasp high on top of my head. Appraising her arrangement, Ruby stood back for the full effect. "Silvy, I do believe you're the prettiest girl I ever did see. That lovely high forehead, so noble"—just the two of us at the bathroom mirror, fixing me up to go off with Uncle Kurt, while Ruby admired what I considered my worst feature. I was excited and certain about myself until I was seated on the worn leather seat of the old Chrysler, and Uncle Kurt looked down on me with frank approval, which made my mind go blank. Nothing I knew about would interest him. I discovered a small stain on my skirt, to spoil my mint condition, and for a few blocks I rode with my hand spread to cover it. I could always make a mountain out of a molehill.

We drove out onto the main highway, swaying in barge-like dignity. When we'd turned up into the hills on the narrow and winding road, it lost its center dividing line, the river behind us now part of the sky, gray in sheeting rain. I'd been alone with Uncle Kurt before. Once, when everyone else went to a movie I'd helped him study, calling out phrases like *"habeas corpus,"* and *"reductio ad absurdum,"* not even saying them right, though Uncle Kurt knew all their definitions anyway. Now, in the rain-dark day, the world washing away outside the windows, *"reductio ad absurdum"* repeated itself in my head like a song.

It helped when Uncle Kurt turned on the radio and Patsy Cline was singing "South of the Border" and I could hum along. There were gardens planted in that wilderness now, evidence that people could live out there in the hills, corn-tasseled, green pumpkins trailed on vines among the rows. Lines of wash dripped glumly in back yards and fleets of rusty school buses were corraled for the summer. We passed rail fences tangled with honeysuckle and roses, and then there were elderberry bushes overhanging the car. When I said, "Ruby would like those for a pie," Uncle Kurt screeched to a stop in the middle of the road. "You don't mind if I wait here." He laughed, speeding up the car while I still had my mouth open.

Up on one of the hills there was a small graveyard, fenced in with iron, the stones buckling and marred, tilting out of the thin grass and streaming rain as though they'd endured an earthquake or a rapture. It seemed the world's most forsaken place. Pringles would be there, Madisons, Pottses, and Adamses, the stillborn babies, wives dead in childbirth, children taken by measles. Ruby's people were probably nearby, and someday she would be too. I asked Uncle Kurt if she missed living in her old home in the mountains. Right then it seemed like pining for an open grave.

"Mom doesn't look back, Silvy," he said. "She's too full of life for that, shining out every day where she is. Don't know how you two came to be so alike"—his smile on me shifting like river light, with the rain beginning to lift.

I didn't say anything after that, not daring to be as happy as I felt outright, but musing on it. I began to take particular notice of the moles that sprinkled Uncle Kurt's arms, little round pepper dots against his pale skin, webbed by the long black hairs that crisscrossed in patterns, as if he'd combed them that way. As if he'd arranged himself for me to love him.

"See that white house on the ridge? That's where Mom was born. And Granny's still right there, where she's always been. Where she belongs." I could tell he liked things staying the same, saying it in a firm, battling kind of voice.

"Who takes care of her?" I knew Granny was almost a hundred years old.

"You'll see. Granny doesn't need much care. Her grandnephew Bill Morris and his wife, Nora, live with her. In her house. They have for a long time. Granny's still more help than care, giving them a home all these years." His teeth behind tightened lips showed in a row like steel buttons.

When we turned up the drive, Granny, coming out of the faded house, seemed mostly a collection of bones tied up in an apron, but her pure white hair flowed from her head, a fountain of protein caught with antique tortoiseshell combs.

"Why, Kurt," she said after peering at him awhile, everybody there now chiming in: "Guess who this is, Auntie. Guess who's come to call." Bill and Nora circled around her, taking care to put words in her mouth, acting as if at any moment she was going to break in half.

"I'm right glad, right glad." Granny gave Uncle Kurt a dry, hissing kiss, staring around then, looking at me and away, saying in a lost, sorry voice, "Where's my Ruby?" They told her Ruby couldn't come, but Granny didn't seem to understand, wandering back into the house. In the detachment of her face I felt as though the rest of us were wreathed in wisps of fog and floating, like those over the ravine.

Uncle Kurt sat in the living room and talked with Bill about the rain, gardens, the railroad. Bill had been a railroad man for over twenty years, ever since his brother had been sealed up in a mine disaster in 1933 and he'd vowed he'd rather starve than have the same thing happen to him. I went to the kitchen and helped set the table, laying out the heavy plates on worn oilcloth, strong reds, orange, and a fawn yellow, the flatware that was both oversized and lightweight at the same time. At least Joey's father wasn't dead. I wondered if he wrote Joey from wherever he had gone, if he wanted him to visit.

During dinner Granny kept getting up and down, the way Ruby did, only Uncle Kurt didn't try to stop her, probably fig-uring some habits are here to stay. She kept asking him did he want more of her fried chicken and dumplings, or the bread-

and-butter pickles she'd put up. Or didn't he always prefer the watermelon, come to remember? A satisfied look came over her face when he ate a slice of each pie she'd made, cherry and gooseberry.

In the front room, where we sat to recover, the furniture seemed uneasy, unpinned, and levitating over the slick plaid linoleum, each arm presenting a tatted doily. I felt queasy, afraid if I made for the open door I'd wobble and lurch, almost seasick. Lace curtains stood starch-stiff at the windows and the fern in the wicker hamper still thrived after fifty years. We sighed, burdened with pie and time. Repeated how good everything was; only Ruby could rival Granny's pie baking. Bill went on about the mines some more, in a thin whine, as though he bored himself, while beside me on the couch, Nora whispered how Granny was failing. "You can't notice it, seeing her like this. But I tell you it's terrible. She'll break her hip and lay there if no one's to home. Burn the house to the ground. Last week it was only the dog that saved us." That dog must have been the one tied at the back of the yard. Surrounded by mounds of dirt and holes tunneled to nowhere and back, its life seemed dedicated to futile attempts at escape.

Uncle Kurt stared from across the room, his mouth pale, eyes aglow like the coal Bill hated so much. He didn't appear to be listening while Bill talked, not that Bill seemed to notice. I'd seen Uncle Kurt sit in a room full of people talking, reading a book, turning the pages as if he were alone. Now, under his gaze, Nora twitched her mouth, eyes flitting everywhere, passing his on the fly, yanking at her permed gray-brown curls as if she'd straighten them by hand. But she didn't stop going on about Granny, something spiteful in her single-mindedness. She said she thought Granny would be a whole lot happier around people her own age. "I know I would." She stuck her chin out.

Granny, in her rocker at the window, stared into the wet woods of the hollow. Once she spoke: "Kurt, you put me in mind of

Mr. Southworth," her voice as distant and formal as her habit of calling her husband by his surname, making you think at first she was referring to a stranger. The tales about him were peculiar, the kind Ruby wouldn't repeat, although I'd heard about him in snatches from different relatives. About him throwing bowls of hot soup when he got wild, anything he could reach sailing through the air. So crazy jealous they'd had to rope and tie him when they took him away to the state hospital, where they couldn't do a thing for him until he burned himself alive in bed. Maybe Nora thought Granny had the same thing in mind for them.

The dog barked and Uncle Kurt stood up, starting for the door after he'd pulled Granny close in his arms. He said he'd see her next time, right there where she belonged. Abrupt, as though he'd been reading a book and had it finished. Granny and the others followed along to the car, Granny whispering that she hoped the Lord would take her, though at the last she seemed to forget she wanted to die. "You come see me right soon, Kurt. Bring your sweet gal." She pinched my cheek, all mixed up, though my cheeks bloomed red as a sweetheart's. Uncle Kurt didn't say a word to anyone else, the engine firing before I got in the car. I'd heard Nora mutter to Bill, "I'd like to see him have to take her."

Driving home we took up both sides of the road, making the curves just barely, taking chances as if Uncle Kurt didn't care about living or dying either. I was afraid to look at him or speak, in case I'd make him more angry, and I pressed myself up against the door and hung on. It felt as though I were riding with that crazy Mr. Southworth, the part of him that Granny saw in Uncle Kurt, and was maybe in his eyes that came searching into people, or even in the fine spread of moles upon his arms. I could still hear Granny's papery voice praying for release.

When we sped into the hotel lot, Uncle Kurt braked hard, pitching me forward against the arm he stuck out in front to catch me. I fumbled at the door handle, but he kept his hand clamped there, making a bar across to hold me in. "Uncle Kurt," I gasped, my head lowered to hide my face.

In a second he laughed, high-pitched, abject, snapped off as he snapped the handle and let the door fall open and bounce clumsily on the hinges. I was out and up the stairs, still hearing its groan.

Joey's mother answered the phone. She said Joey was at work and I went ahead, out of breath and nervous, giving her the message, even if she did think I was fast, running after a boy, maybe even like the woman that took away her husband. I said Joey should call me, or come by. If he wasn't busy.

After supper I waited for him out on the porch, pacing up and down, wondering if he'd come or even call, the rug squishing under my feet, the cushions sodden with rain. Uncle Kurt had been sleeping when he was called to eat, and since he was leaving early in the morning, I thought maybe I wouldn't have to see him. It was clearing over the river, the sun out from the clouds in time to bid farewell, dusty pink and silver polishing up the sky, the water rippling as though it were coming all apart. The elms over the river walk hung limp from their dousing. I hadn't taken the time to fix myself up and wondered whether I looked as disheveled, if Joey would think I'd spent the day out on the porch waiting for him. That is if he wanted to see me, if he bothered to come.

Then Uncle Kurt stepped out on the porch and stood by the railing, gazing out over the river that had been beautiful a long time. Around his eyes I noticed pricks of strain when he smiled, seeming to like me again, but before we had to say anything, a car roared in the alley. Joey came striding into view, keys dangling in his hand—a look in his eye for me. Like both of us were done fooling around and were going to get serious, come hell or high water.

He came onto the porch, solid and deliberate, with his own brand of style, politely shaking hands with Uncle Kurt, nodding to me. Against the white of his shirt, the veins of his arms stood out swollen and swarthy. His lank brown hair was combed back wet and sleek. For once I'd be the one telling him how nice he looked. From three feet away I could feel his back under my hands, its muscled pathways and swooping hollows.

"Good night, goodbye," we called, and Joey and I went along the brick walk under the elms to get in the car. From the street, sitting close in his mother's coupe, turning toward the highway, I looked back once more to see Uncle Kurt, who had thrilled me to death. Around him and above, the curving porches and towers of the white Victorian edifice arched up high, like the wind-filled sails of the ships that used to run the great Ohio, and he, a dark entrancing captain, stood at the wheel, sighting for grandmothers, elderberries, and souls.

Jack Pine Savage

THE PIERCING-EYED HUNTERS in the birch canoe, wrought
by the painter of the frontispiece into an extension of the plunging
rapids, still faced Paul when the return of Geneva's car snapped
him back to reality, back to Wednesday evening in the suburbs,
Geneva home from her French lesson. Farewell *les bons
hommes*—he tipped the last of his brandy and closed the book.
When he stood up he had to lean briefly on his chair to extract
himself from what felt like a permanent right angle. Age would
have finished him as Québecois long before. He navigated the
throw rugs on the slick floor and headed north to the kitchen,
envisioning Ste. Anne de Beaupré and a host of heavenly angels
hovering over the continent, as once his mother had convinced
him they thronged his attic room. The car door closed as he
closed in on the brandy, feeling its pull like the poles, the waves
of tundra lapping the barrens, the old North of unbounded cold,
province of ravens, plateaus of moss, source bed of glaciers.
Sometimes it seemed enough to have come this far, north of
Albany to the jumping-off place of the modern world. If ever it
became too much, he could go that way, the way of trappers
and prospectors. Find a haven in the logging camps. He was a

big man and still strong—once he worked out the kinks. His hands muscled from more than holding a pencil. A veritable jack pine savage. And when he'd had the course they could bury him over there in the old way, under a heap of slag on open ground.

As Geneva entered the mudroom on the front of the house, Paul slipped back into his chair. "Hello," she called out, hangers singing on the rod, the vibrato of her low voice appealing. When she poked her gray-black curls around the corner, Paul waved, answering her smile. His own formidable praline, curvy in the beige wool skirt she'd worn in high school, although her boots were practically army issue with the stout tread her doctor recommended as insurance against another fall. Her bones sometimes looked transparent to Paul, but that was his fancy, as though he had X-ray eyes. In fact, her condition was responding to treatment and the prescribed regimen. He wished he wasn't sitting there lifting a snifter of brandy, like some stubborn teenager; and besides, they couldn't afford it. Not with all the lessons: tap dancing, horns, batons, French.

Sometimes his cozy bungalow reminded him of those clocks he'd seen in Germany, every quarter hour some stagy performer swinging out to dance the hootchy-koo. The children needed clothes, needed everything you could name, and then some. The house too was in a continual upheaval of refurbishing and remodeling, Geneva tireless in search of optimal efficiency—to save the children embarrassment in front of their friends. Further embarrassment, from what Paul could ascertain, seeing them suffer the torment of being alive. He'd had his own troubles: a lisp throughout grammar school, hair the texture of raffia. Though in those days, suffering was considered ennobling, and the effort to avoid it unavailing at best. In plain sight he walked over to top off his brandy. This one he'd savor, let it take him through into the dark. Maybe if he'd had some lessons when he was a kid on South Wabash.

"Snowing yet?" he called to Geneva, his lady fair. It was a

comfortable subject, an enthusiasm they shared, though for different reasons. Paul was a romantic, while for Geneva the raging of a tempest set her teeth; even at that moment she might bring out her insulation tape and put her palm to the wall as though to a human heart. They'd beat around the bush awhile, neither of them prepared to talk about Ike. Not yet.

"A few flakes. It's beginning." She continued to bustle, picking up wraps, ordering the boots to dry on the rack over the heating vent, wiping runnels off the gleaming pine floor. She'd refinished it by hand, crawling with sandpaper and steel wool, no doubt while he was getting his beauty rest. Alone. So many days victory had seemed within his grasp: the children at school, his classes called, or perhaps he was home with a cold. Whatever she was doing could wait, it seemed to him, and after bald hints were exhausted he'd proposition her point-blank to come with him to bed. The extent of her surprise shamed him, and even if she acquiesced, the conquest fell flat. Maybe he'd be less horny if he scythed all day in the fields of the Lord. "Want a drink?" he ventured as she whisked by to broom up some ashy debris by the wood stove. Her narrow nose, dead-white with cold, glanced as though it could deliver a paper cut.

"No thanks, dear." Of course she wanted one. Who didn't? But one of them at least could tighten her belt. When they pored over the budget, to squeeze out another plum, perhaps a flute or a viburnum bush, his self-indulgence took the limelight. It had helped when he gave up downhill skiing, contenting himself with cross-country. He'd traded in his golf clubs for a fishing rod. Cigarettes fell by the wayside, almost entirely, in that desperate time when they'd made their break with collegiate life, minus tenure, and moved East, where Paul took the only job he could get, teaching history at a private academy. They'd nearly foundered on reduced circumstances, coming close to sending Geneva and the children back to stay with her sister. He still had his pipe, God bless it, clinging like a babe.

"It's picking up," Geneva said, lifting the curtain to peer outside. Earlier I saw the northern lights. I stopped to watch." The soul of a poet resided in that industrious hausfrau. Her parents, missionaries to the Inuit, as she'd taught him to call the Eskimo, had named her Freyja Geneva, calling up their lonesomeness and European exile, their spirit of accommodation. But their deaths when she was still an infant had left her a name that was her sole hold on her parents' adventurousness, on her own emergence in the colder latitudes among the reindeer troops. That image captivated Paul when they first met at a USO dance, Geneva across the room with her lifted chin, the ligaments of her throat arched and bared from her slenderness, exposing her winsome clavicle. That tension, the clash of force and tenderness, drew him toward her. There was still something pure, sparkling, and inviolate about her, and as she entered the room he smelled the snowy night, the resin of pine. He reached to touch her fleetingly as she gathered and straightened the papers he'd discarded by his chair, her dark head at his knee bobbing like a poodle's.

"*Parlez-vous français?*" he stuttered, shy about his accent, a slough of sloth before the Snow Queen. It would have taken so little for him to tidy up, and if he'd gone to the garage, even just to look around, greeting her with a flange of nails in his teeth, how he would have encouraged her. Although it had been only the winter before that Geneva had stood two hours in dark cold, holding a light while he strained to finish cutting a foundation window, a project she had convinced him would take less than an hour. She had ended up in bed with back strain, while Paul kicked himself around the block and renewed his vow to resist her forever. Shamefaced, he regarded her from the armchair, though she was the one on her knees.

"I just love it, Paul. And it's coming so fast." Geneva would never show off to him, but she was proud of herself, beginning at last to speak the language of her parents in their service to the church. "When we go to Montreal we'll fit right in." He imagined them crossing the border, then going on, clear to the Arctic Circle, where she'd spent her first two weeks of life ruffed to the earlobes in ermine. But that was his dream more than hers, Geneva content to wear serviceable woolens, trading pleasantries with Mademoiselle behind the desk at the Bonaventure. She would have liked him to learn French along with her and the other housewives, in spite of the extra expense, his excuse. In the logging camps he'd have to learn fast, pointing and grunting, begging for mercy. Furtively, he sometimes perused the vocabulary pinned on the refrigerator door, holding his breath, as though he might discover it already within himself, as when he was a boy he'd figured the priests were born with Latin. Poor Geneva, her husband was as grotesque and unmanageable as a drowned horse tumbling and pitching in floodwaters, stiffened with obstinance. In the old days they had used horses in the camps to move the logs down to the rivers.

"You can serve as my interpreter, Gigi."

"Oh no, I'll never be good. Not really. It's mostly a gesture, something to do. The French are so insecure. They cut you dead if you don't speak the language, but probably in another generation it'll be gone and everybody will use English."

Her predictable modesty, together with the unbidden note of prerogative, made him smile. Missionaries did have some success eradicating the old customs, notably revenge murder. Such optimism was probably the last best hope for mankind, coming down squarely on the side of self-control and morality, the lessons of his childhood Catholicism, left so long ago on South Wabash. But not entirely dispensed with—abandon them at your peril. After all, he had not been able to wrestle his doctoral thesis to a satisfactory conclusion, no matter his lifelong interest in American civilization—or the lack thereof. He could find excuses: endless projects, two growing children, Geneva's illness. But in the end it came down to his own confusion.

His immigrant parents had never moved from the house where he'd been born, and his sister lived on in that sarcophagus, without upstairs heat even in Chicago, the bathroom still the drafty converted storeroom off the kitchen. When he and Geneva returned to visit, they declared their independence by staying at the Holiday Inn. No one had ever been happy in that house, certainly not after the older, favored son of the family died of scarlet fever when Paul was seven. His memories, infrequent and scant, mostly of his mother reclining on the downstairs daybed, frayed green cloth shades pulled to the sill, pinpricks of light, like point lace, tracing midday constellations, the sibilance of rosary beads slipping round. Paul had made his bid for freedom: the armed services, G.I. Bill for the family's first college graduate, his reprobate marriage to a Protestant. For all the good it did, ending up pretty much where he'd begun. He'd read that the early French traders had seldom spent more than a week a year on the outside, the rest of their days lived among pines and savages, winters of unbroken white.

Geneva, setting the coffee table to rights, maintained her Victorian bearing, a painted dish in her lap—the requisite nude camouflaged among the ruminant deer. Her paper towel circled the glass, almost idly, as though her thoughts strayed. When she was finished, she'd ask about Ike. Paul wondered why he'd confessed, after his return from Germany. It had been wartime—no questions asked. Geneva had heard him out, her chin lifted, and there wasn't a word about breaking their engagement. Just the break in her voice, a hoarse catch that was one of her evanescent charms, told him that he had hurt her. Selfishly, unnecessarily. He imagined blurting out, "For God's sake, Geneva. You should never have married me. I'm not good enough." Suffocated, he realized he'd been holding his breath.

She settled back on the cushions and asked, "Did you talk to Ike?" No, he hadn't, and what of it. He decided he would have another brandy before bed.

"He went right down after eating, Gigi. He's got a test." Homework the perfect excuse. He envied Ike, although when he envisioned his attic cubicle on South Wabash, the torn wallpaper, a hush from below, camphor permeating the air from soaked cotton balls suspended over the heating vents in the kitchen, it loomed like a sanitarium.

"They sent out the schedule today. His team has the pool from five to six, beginning tomorrow morning. I called the school before I left." Her sob caught at him, though he knew she wasn't even aware of the note in her voice. She herself was ready to do what had to be done, as her parents had set about converting the native population. "We warned him about this, Paul. He knows how we feel."

Paul was no match for her, with his equivocal morbidity. Again he saw himself as a swollen corpse, lurching out of roiling water beneath a level sky. All around a profound emptiness. One summer Paul had taken Geneva to a remote Northern lake, as far as you could get in Michigan, to show her a preserve of ancient spruce, hundreds of years old, high, massive, in a formal and majestic setting. In the clear lake tiny colored stones appeared to line the bottom with iridescent scales, as though the water were swimming away. Geneva had stood transfixed in the groove that cut through the center of two stands, a narrow channel of waving grass, flourishing like canebrake. Her eyes glazed with scattered shadow, black hair tarnished green and twined around her sapling throat. He took her face in his hands and she slid beneath him into the grass, where they glided like swans, while above them the wind cleaved the boughs. Afterward there were no tears or demands, Geneva as certain with her gift as though she held it in her hands. He had left her and gone away to war, to Germany and all that happened there. It had never been quite the same between them, and now their antique sleigh bed at the top of the house, dimpled in its poplin duvet, seemed in harness, bearing them inexorably to their long winter's nap.

Paul mumbled, talking over the empty pipe clenched in his teeth. "I could go on and keep doing it. I don't really mind that much." He let his head hang, the plea pathetic, contradicting everything they'd settled before, when he had been savage. Yelling, "I can't do it for another session. I'll strangle him. I'm too old to get up every day in pitch-dark," the memory of the coal scuttle and long-ago dark mornings reverberating in him, his father firing the furnace before he left to distribute the morning papers to the waiting trucks. Paul had meant what he said, at the time, recalling vividly the milk carton he hurled at the wall before Christmas break, when Ike had kept him waiting at the pool until he'd missed a class. Another time he'd slapped Ike across the face, back and forth, daring him to run to his mamma. He wondered if similar scenes were enacted in the privacy of other cars tooting toward the Sportsdome in dawn's early light, similar crimes. If just one other kid lived anywhere near their end of town there'd be another parent to share the driving. One more year would do it. Then Ike would be sixteen—he'd lend him the car.

But there was more to it: Ike at fifteen was still one of the pack, placing fifth and sixth when he was lucky, and his diving trials didn't even count. If he was going to be the next Mark Spitz or make any kind of Olympic team, he should have been winning, taking first in the valley, the state. It didn't look good. Who was going to say, "Sorry, kid. You gave it all you've got but you're not going to make it. Start making other plans"? He and Geneva had told themselves this was one way to begin getting the message across, but Paul was waffling. Why couldn't he just keep driving the boy until he was ready to see for himself.

"I feel the same as before." Geneva didn't lower her voice and Paul got the notion that maybe Ike had heard them all along and was playing dumb to get back at them. But more probably he'd blocked out the sound of their voices, beating them down with his monstrous incantation—the greatest, the greatest.

"You can't do it, Paul. It's winter term. If I could help." She looked down at her hands, which had the gloss of clear starch. He recalled his mother rinsing shirts in galvanized washtubs, her hands large and work-worn. "When we were younger it was okay, but it's taking a toll on the family. I feel you scarcely see Debbie." His mercurial twelve-year-old, who had forsaken him for pals her own age, even right then off in the neighborhood. Occasionally he wondered about Hannah, if she thought of him. If she'd expected him to write, although they'd agreed not to. They hadn't any future.

"I don't really sleep either, Paul. After you get up. I lie there resting, but it's hard on everybody."

"Especially Ike." He evened the score. They'd said it all before. He thought of the boy, Adam's apple roving his throat, the few beginnings of acne scarring his incandescent skin. In his sharp-angled face, slanted green eyes were feathered by his mother's heavy dark lashes. Why did he have to want something so much, poor devil. Paul stroked the puffs and polyps of his own acne scarring, confined to his neck. It could still amaze him that after what had seemed like eons of activity, the region had become a dormant cone, unlikely to erupt again in his lifetime. To tetracycline—he raised his glass.

"It's just until spring, when he can ride his bike." Geneva and Ike were alike, made of adamant. Though Paul could take credit for Ike's size and strength; not a bad show even if you had to pine in dry-dock.

"He'll be out of it by then," he said. "It's going to finish him for the team." If they were going through with this they shouldn't deceive themselves. He imagined Ike under his Walkman, escaping the voice of doom. Staring at his stocking feet, Paul was aware of a glimmering impulse to lift one smack into Geneva's merganser chin. Set her resolve aquiver. She was right about sticking to their decision, but he wasn't man enough to say so. He whistled a bar of "Moon River," then shut his trap. Geneva was on the nose about that too: he whistled when he was tense, to cover up. Naturally he would be without the joy of song.

Geneva went into the kitchen. At least neither of them said, "This hurts us more than it hurts him." Although sooner was probably better than later. "He'll hate us for a while," Paul said, but not for Geneva to hear. Geneva didn't countenance hate, not in a family.

He listened to her move in the kitchen, preparing the ritual tea, hot enough to scald your tonsils, dark as a mote. She had to be careful, no more canoeing or even yard work. But given an indoor life, rest, and medication, she would probably live to a ripe old age of grandmothering and cozies. Christ, he was nearly fifty.

Waiting for the water to boil, he heard her laying the table for breakfast, the yellow-and-white-checked mats mellow against the oak table, the thick porcelain mugs. Out slid the tea tray, a linen cloth snapped, cream in the pitcher, cookies on a plate. She measured the tea, a ceremony. He could remember listening to his mother in the kitchen, identifying every move. Though for all that vigilance he'd be hard-pressed to fix a decent meal.

When Geneva started toward the stairs with the tray, Paul went into the dining room. He didn't want to hear any of their words coming up through the floor or heating vents. Already he knew Geneva would be planning the purchase of some expensive modish item the boy had wanted, something the others had. Ike would accept it, always polite—who could resist Staffordshire, the elements of style. Standing in the dark before the double glass doors, he turned on the floodlight to watch the world of snow. Sometimes at the pool, he'd see Ike shivering, hunched and blue with cold, his body hair riffed to a pelt. But if Paul approached to ask if he wanted to go home, Ike never seemed to hear the question, as though he were already climbing the rungs to the high board or was lost in the English Channel. Paul, the wind guttering the snow, heard in the hue and cry beyond the window his own unanswered call.

Later, Geneva came with her tray, the teapot snuggled deep in the quilted cozy like a dog in its hat and coat. She wore her glasses; the new bifocals enlarged her eyes, magnifying unmercifully the surrounding lines, and her expression appeared stunned by exaggeration. He imagined grinding the lens to powder under his heel.

"He was pretty much expecting it, I think. Didn't say much. I guess he's okay." For once the appeal in her voice was unaffecting. They'd never hear from Ike, although Paul would come upon shreds of evidence, a snapped pane of glass, dented moldings, fantastically twisted metal rods. Geneva turned away and went to sit on the couch, her set expression in grim contrast with the velveteen bed of roses. "If you'd stop in and say good night, Paul. Remind him about Sunday, skiing with the Shaws." Ike should count his lucky stars that he still had downhill—money no object for some around here.

Geneva began to flip the pages of a catalogue. A digital watch, one-piece body suit, racing skates. The fire in the corner stove shifted down while Paul's chest panted as though he'd been running. She didn't look at him again, but when he stood, her leg stopped shaking. After he saw Ike he'd make his escape to bed, the room to himself. All hell would break loose, he'd open the window. Until she came to bed and shut it—warding off an outbreak of yearning, he sometimes thought.

Ike answered Paul's knock with a noncommittal grunt, and Paul covered his intrusion with a chatty "How's it going," settling himself on the twin bed, cousin to the simulated walnut desk and shelf unit Geneva had selected when Ike entered high school. The boy slumped at his desk, twirling a pencil, while Paul occupied himself filling his meerschaum, although lighting it would have to wait for spring—the house off limits, hermetically sealed for winter. Geneva had spent the entire weekend of

Paul's hunting trip taping the seams of the basement windows, fitting plastic storms behind the insulated drapes, until the room was so cozy Ike wore only briefs and T-shirt, as though he basked in a spa. Some outfit to receive your mother at fifteen. Throughout his own high-school years, Paul had worked seven to eleven at a gas spa, any homework accomplished in the hall between classes. The wind storming his bedroom window inundated his childhood dreams with mayhem. Maybe what Ike was missing on the road to fame and glory was some good old-fashioned extremity and neglect, à la South Wabash. Though Paul was nothing to write home about. When he glanced up over the filled pipe, Ike's dark head, fallen on his book, looked like a matching walnut fitting.

"What are you working on, son?" Paul felt a chill seize the back of his neck, but it could only be the hand of fate in that cocoon. Geneva was probably a throwback—he'd read that igloos were sometimes so stifling the natives cavorted stark naked. "Algebra?"

"Yeah." Ike had come up with a sob of his own. Paul would rather have been pistol-whipped than endure Ike's tears, the last he could remember falling freely when Ike was four and his helium balloon had taken flight. Paul's eyes had filled at the time, that speck of red carrying off rays of his own bright hope.

"The mountain Sunday, hey?" Paul's smile, out of control, seemed mounted about two inches in front of his face. The silent treatment intensified, his pit-bull son patiently closing off his breath until Paul hissed, "I don't want any damn bellyaching around here. Be a man for once. It's time you grew up." The rasping scold from South Wabash, the old man slurping from a soup bowl of coffee, the preferred cup of Alsace-Lorraine. Paul got out at seventeen, enlisted in the service, and sailed for Europe to fight the Big One. Those were heady times, but he paid for any lingering thoughts of Hannah, her smiles at his eagerness; the stab of guilt felt nearly lethal. He touched Ike's shoulder on the way to the door. "I'm counting on you, son. It's us men together."

He accomplished the two flights of stairs to his bedroom in stealth and perturbation. He'd have to think of fresh excuses for retreat, his dawn runs suspended. Any interference this night and he wouldn't be held responsible. Geneva knew what he was made of. Once he'd kissed her, aching, drawing her with him toward their room on an afternoon when both kids had gone to a movie. She had stopped him, pressing his arms to his sides, gripping his elbows. "I'm ashamed," she whispered, moving his hand to feel the brace that strapped her upper body after a sprain. "You wouldn't have anyway," Paul snapped, turning to leave the house.

Tucked safely in bed, he heard Geneva talking on the phone, calling Debbie home. Maybe now he'd have more time for the kid, wouldn't be so wiped out. Although he didn't know exactly what they would do together since she'd become an expert on hairdos. How to distinguish between a flip and a flop. He burrowed deeper into the featherbed, envied the sleeping bears. He couldn't remember asking the old man for a dime. Both of them would have been embarrassed. If he'd been the one who had died, instead of his brother, the favorite—an old prayer from childhood. Any carcass dragged down on the tundra fed first the wolves and bears, then the birds. Last the implacable insects, until there was only bone on the bloodstained snow. Near sleep, he ran with the antelope over the mosses and lichen that cushioned the frozen world. There was a species of alga in the Far North that grew in snow, turned it red. No doubt the natives had a word for it. Long ago Geneva had bent to his hands, breathing in tremendous gulps, burying her nose again and again, murmuring how she loved their smell. He felt her tongue on his dripping fingers and in a dream carried her endlessly through fields of crimson snow.

In the morning Ike was gone from his room and, then they

realized, the house. Had he run off, ruining their lives as they'd ruined his? Paul struggled into trousers, yanking them over his pajamas, heading for the car, when Geneva said, "You know what he's done, I bet. He walked."

He heard her on the phone, calling the school. From the way she thanked the secretary, he knew Ike had made practice, gotten there safely. Paul went to stand in the kitchen doorway, where Geneva stood at the sink looking out the window, her back to him bare to the waist in the nightgown, pale with its frail winged scapulae. It seemed years since she had wanted him to see her naked body, and when he turned and went quickly to their room, he felt as though he skulked through his own home.

On his way to the academy, following the path plowed through a wood bordering the campus, Paul imagined Ike taking the route earlier, before the plow, several more miles to go. He must have set his alarm for three, to make it on time, his sturdy well-muscled body thrusting through drifts and into the wind. Now he'd be in Algebra, Latin and History to come. Paul caught himself humming, stopped, and then continued. "The melody haunts my reverie," louder. During the day he planned to write out cards for Ike to carry with him, to help memorize vocabulary, dates, and formulas. Maybe he'd drive him once or twice a week and together they'd see it through. He knew from experience that you could put in years and years in a classroom, when your heart lay elsewhere.

His arrival home found the family waiting for him to sit down to dinner. Lasagna, one of his favorites, and he tried to read in Geneva's face that it was for him. But she seemed withdrawn, serving the plates with downcast eyes, and the kids were subdued, their napkins in their laps. "Hey, good-looking." He love-pinched Debbie's thin cheek, her baby fat so rapidly disappearing. She used to beg him to play cards, although he doubted she would shriek so gleefully now when he was caught with the Old Maid. For all he knew, it was sexist. He'd have to

come up with something. Ike looked half dead, reminded Paul
of himself on those early mornings at the pool, slumped against
the tiles at the top of the bleachers. Amid the cavernous echoes,
the winter light teal blue beyond the arched glass roof, he'd
sometimes felt he hung suspended in a hot-air balloon, while far
below ancient rivalry was unloosed beneath his feet.

"Isaac." Geneva's severity, along with her voice's undercurrent sobbing, summoned all their eyes. Her plate lay untouched,
and when Paul lowered his fork, his hand was shaking. They
hadn't talked all day and he didn't know what she would say,
what she would do. "Do you have any idea how selfish that was.
For you to leave the house like that, without a word to anyone.
You can't do it, Ike. Look at you, you're falling asleep in your
plate." She was certain again, after the fright they'd had. "That's
the trouble with sports. Children grow up thinking the world
revolves around them, expecting life will always go their way.
Well, it doesn't." With her lifted chin and trembling lips, Geneva
looked like a disappointed child herself, bearing up. Debbie's
eyes brimmed with the quick tears of a sister's loyalty to her
older brother. No matter their private feuds.

In the silence after Geneva spoke, they went on eating, sad
and forlorn, Paul's eyes fastened on Debbie's still flattened in-
fantine fingers as she folded her napkin into a fan. The plastic
sheeting over the window languished in the wind. He remembered how once he'd seized the day, idly fashioning a creation
from his napkin, and then, on impulse, using a wire tie as a
band, clipped the affair to his collar. His family looked up to
discover him at the head of the table in a red bow tie, on his
face the angelic piety of a choirboy. Their former hilarity rang
in his ears as now he regarded them, sullen and betrayed. Reflected in the dark window before him, the table scene appeared
suspended from his neck like a millstone. He surprised himself
too when he blurted out, "How about a swim, kids? Right after
we eat. If your mother agrees." Geneva removed her glasses

before she returned his gaze, her eyes soft and candlelighted. With a word he had been forgiven and would be trusted, even in the dark world.

Debbie was out of her seat and into his lap while Paul explained his inspiration. He could take both of them to the pool every evening after dinner. Not for long, so they'd have time for homework. But that way Ike could get in some laps, stay in shape, and be ready to join the team again in the spring. Paul felt like a miracle worker, Ike apologizing to his mother for scaring them, asking her forgiveness, then bolting his meal and asking to be excused. He stuffed rolls in his pocket and hurried to get ready, swearing he was too tired to study anyway and would do it in the morning. Debbie nuzzled Paul's whiskers, the way she used to, before following Ike. Possibly she'd develop a passion for the sport, although his memory of her in a bikini and high-heeled bathing clogs, already one hip thrust forward, made him think he'd have other worries. But for then he luxuriated, Geneva eating peaceably, banked by candles, smiling dimly in his direction.

"It's such a good idea, Paul. Really nice for both of them." The inclusion of Debbie won her heart, appealing to her sense of fairness, no favorites. It must have rankled her, raised along with her aunt's children, not belonging in the same way. Geneva still denied wanting anything special for herself, even new clothes. She made do with old things, letting down hems and altering necklines. He could see her in pigtails, austere and proud, dreading the slightest implication that she would take what rightfully belonged to others.

"Maybe sometimes you'll ride along, Gigi." Sensitive to her feelings, Paul added quickly, "We'll sit and spoon," although swimming was actually supposed to be good for her condition. It had occurred to him that ultimately the ancient struggle between them might be reducible to a matter of hormones. She nodded, getting up to bring out flour and sugar to make cookies for their return, finding her way to be part of things—they'd probably be treated to frosted porpoises and starfish.

The children were milling in the doorway, watching everything, and Paul didn't feel free to kiss Geneva the way he wanted to. She would stiffen under their surveillance. But later she might be waiting in the dark, tucked in on his side by the night table, her hand out to warn him. A proposition he found invariably arousing, even though it was always her call. Above her head on the pine rail the painted plates were vintage Currier and Ives, each a domestic tableau with dreamy-eyed oxen, good-humored, obedient children going about their chores. In his earmuffs and woolen scarf Paul felt as yoked and homely. The modern twist— he was the one doing chores.

Outside, the lamps were low, with the snow piled high, winding paths sparkling in and out from houses aglow in Christmas wreaths and bows. The stars hung at intervals, as though on a staff to be sung for the glory of God. The distance between himself in the front driving and his children giggling and tussling in the rear seemed as preordained, notes in the song of life. Before the highway liquor store a high bank of snow pooled red in the lighted neon. On the way back he might stop for a foreign beer, the poor man's reward.

Fatigue overcame Paul as soon as he entered the Sportsdome, shades of the morning watch. Maybe he'd doze off while the kids swam, his dinner a plummet at his waist, his life more than half spent. Canoe men had generally died well before mid-life, victims of chance, disease, and grueling work. The French had taken to the wild, north-flowing rivers, like savages, voyaging in canoes of papery birch-bark layered over ribs of white cedar. Along the rapids, they tracked the canoes, attaching them to ropes drawn by men on shore. On portages they had run for miles, stooped low from the burdening packs and canoes, following a chain of water bridging the St. Lawrence to the western ocean. If his brother had lived, they might have fled together over the same route, beyond railroads, outposts, and tamaracks, adopting the native's stingy mustache à la Fu Manchu.

The pool was no place to relax, kids everywhere frisking and dripping. From time to time Debbie's blue-capped head surfaced, bobbing for his smile. A poor affair, it seemed to Paul, but she spent her time angling for it, as though his seeing her in the water meant more than being there. Maybe that was what sports did for a person. Ike never seemed to give him a thought, striving back and forth in his lane, self-willed, self-absorbed, his mother's nemesis. Probably the next time Debbie would decline to come along, fast working her way up another ladder, to prom queen.

He waved to her and let himself out into the cooler corridor, lighting up a Kent. How could he give them up—cigarettes, brandy, and his trench coat had brought him through the war. It was stale, from a crumpled pack he kept for the occasional backslide, but he savored it after the initial light-headedness. He might read too, something that could make him uneasy at home, old spit-and-polish on her feet till she dropped. Smoking, he leaned against the beige tile, alone except for two kids at the candy machine and the girl in the ticket booth knitting. Her angora sweater feathered her cheek with each breath, her tongue sliding between her teeth in concentration, knit, purl. It seemed to rise from a place as warm and fomenting as the watery domain beyond the double doors, her lips some color like melon or pomegranate. The natives had been generous with their women, at least with the French, who had asked only to live as they did, spending themselves and moving on. Using what was at hand, laying up nothing for the morrow. The girl behind the counter looked up, directly at Paul. Her flush rose as his own hit like a needle in the arm.

He moved rapidly down the hall to the skating rink, which was closed to the public for private lessons. Down below on the ice a young girl stood poised, dressed in a dark leotard and leg warmers. She was waiting for music, he assumed, although he didn't hear it when she began her swooping glide, reeling out turns and spins, as part of a continuous chain. Her figures, dissolving and collapsing in upon themselves, burst out with the expanding distance, as if she created space for herself out of motion and possession. Her blades drove the ice, sparks dying into the light. Use me, use me.

Bent over and stamping out his cigarette, Paul flinched when Ike came up suddenly beside him. He wore his coat, bundled up for the cold. Paul couldn't speak, his throat swollen, but Ike was preoccupied, shifting, stretching like a dog about to yawn, his green eyes cloudy. Getting ready to reveal something Paul dreaded. One of those annoying and puzzling revelations calculated to injure. He could sense malice, as if it crested within himself. Why did the boy have to be like that, brimming with reprehensible urges, stiff-necked intentions. Paul faced the ice, the girl now walking over to her coach, rubbing one knee. With her luck she probably had a chauffeur in livery and a live-in masseuse.

"Dad, it's no good like this. Coming at night. Without the others I can't get going. It's not the same. I'm sorry, Dad." Ike said it fast, ending with a gulp. Paul stared ahead, hiding the shame in his eyes, the pitiable excess of his own lost hopes. The preposterous longing that Ike would ever be anything more than this, a middle-aged man lurking in desire on the far side of a glass.

He heard Ike's voice going on beside him, a younger Ike, someone Paul hadn't heard from in a long time, and he listened awhile just to the sound, only gradually taking in what he was saying. "I wasn't going to make it anyhow. It wasn't in the cards. Let's face it, Dad." Ike's grin when Paul looked over shivered into a gulp. "I guess I let you and Mom down."

Paul turned away again; the boy was his mother's son. Raised among strangers, she displayed under all circumstances the inherent deference due to honored benefactors. The ice blurred before his eyes in a powdery red mist, the girl skating in a spotlight that seemed to color the whole world. He reached out and ruffled Ike's hair, noticing they were nearly the same height; forced himself: "You're the greatest." His hand came away tacky with pool water and a stray hair glistened on his palm. Without their women, the French had lost touch, eating the raw kill, following the migrations and rivers in the old way, lying down on the cold ground to die young.